Lucky Dogs,

Lost Hats, and

Dating Don'ts

Lucky Dogs,
Lost Hats, and
Dating Don'ts

Hi-Lo Stories about Real Life

Thomas Fish, Ph.D. & Jillian Ober, M.A., CRC

proving
press

Photo Credits:

Jillian Ober—pp. 1, 4, 6, 8, 15, 17, 21, 26, 28, 30, 41, 55, 60, 62, 69, 71, 73, 77, 79, 85, 90, 97, 100, 105, 109, 115, 119, 121, 123, 151, 155, 162, 165, 166, 189, 191, 199, 201, 206, 209, 212

J.J. Jordan—pp. 13, 43, 49, 50, 52, 58, 103, 112, 137, 139, 141, 148, 169, 173, 181, 203

Michelle Long—pp. 127, 176

Lauren Fish—p. 134

p. 3—"Heavy snow with freezing fog," © 2008, JimsFlicker, used under a Creative Commons Attribution License: http://creativecommons.org/licenses/by/2.0/deed.en

p. 25—http://www.city-data.com

p. 88—"Vancouver, BC," © 2010, Maya-Anaïs Yataghène, used under a Creative Commons Attribution License: http://creativecommons.org/licenses/by/2.0/deed.en

p. 183—"Oh what a day," © 2010, Rachel Kramer, used under a Creative Commons Attribution License: http://creativecommons.org/licenses/by/2.0/deed.en

p. 210—"Fiore's Deli @ eire and Oakley," © 2006, Chad Magiera, used under a Creative Commons Attribution License: http://creativecommons.org/licenses/by/2.0/deed.en

Paperback ISBN: 978-1-63337-768-4
eBook ISBN: 978-1-63337-769-1

Dedication

To our friend Steve for his belief in everyone's right to learn

Table of Contents

Acknowledgments

Words of thanks never truly suffice. But, with that said, we are sincerely grateful to the following people who helped us develop and polish these stories: Dr. Paula Rabidoux, Dr. Amy Shuman, Tammy Bailey, and Brock Kingsley. These individuals provided invaluable guidance and enthusiasm throughout the course of this project. We are also thankful to Serena Dempsey and J.J. Jordan for their input and help securing photographs. In addition, our administrative assistant, Michelle Long, has been a steady source of help and we are grateful to her.

Inspiration for this project was provided by our long-time friend and former student intern, Anke Gros-Kunkel and her colleagues at the University of Cologne in Germany. Anke and her colleagues generously shared short stories they developed, and critiqued our stories.

A number of focus groups were conducted to determine the topics and direction of this project. We are grateful to Lou Venerri for skillfully conducting these focus group sessions and analyzing the responses. We are also grateful to the people with disabilities, family members, and professionals who participated in the groups.

Funding for this project was provided in part by The Columbus Foundation. We are particularly grateful to Emily Savors from The Columbus Foundation for her continuing support of the Next Chapter Book Club over the past nine years.

We appreciate the assistance from Nancy Gray Paul at Woodbine House in editing and refining our work. She has been a pleasure to work with, and her belief in the project has been unyielding.

Jillian would like to thank her mother, Pamela Cable, for demonstrating her love for writing as she pursued and at last accomplished her dream of publishing her first novel.

Lastly, we want to thank all of our devoted Next Chapter Book Club members, affiliates, and volunteers. They are the reason these short stories were written.

Introduction

"Never doubt that a small group of individuals can change the world."

—Margaret Meade

Interesting and enjoyable short stories for teens and adults with reading challenges. Go figure! This collection of short stories is a result of our experience with the Next Chapter Book Club (NCBC), a community-based book club program for people with intellectual and developmental disabilities (IDD). Since 2002, NCBC has provided weekly opportunities for hundreds of people with IDD to read and learn together, talk about books, and make friends in a fun, community setting. Established at The Ohio State University Nisonger Center, NCBC has grown from two initial clubs to over 200 worldwide. Often times the simplest ideas have the most profound effects. NCBC is one of those ideas.

Much like any other book club, NCBC members choose which books they would like to read. Members have read everything from adapted classic novels, such as *The Secret Garden* and *Treasure Island*, to children's books by Beverly Cleary. However, we've struggled to find literature featuring adult characters and adult topics written at a low reading level. We explored offerings in the genre of Hi-Lo fiction and found that most material was primarily written with a young audience in mind. ("Hi-Lo" refers to *high* interest–*low* reading level literature.)

The message from our book club members over the years has been clear: "We want to read more about real life things. We're not kids." So, we wrote this book of short stories in order to cover an array of adult topics in a way that would be understood and enjoyed by people with IDD. Furthermore, we set out to create a book that differs from other Hi-Lo fiction on the market in that it's written with this particular group of adults in mind. In fact, many of the characters in the stories have IDD, although this is not always explicit.

At the start of the project, we conducted a series of focus groups to help guide us in selecting story topics and characters. Focus groups included book club members, parents, and professionals. We were encouraged to keep the stories fun and relatable. Many focus group participants told us that book club members want to read about relationships—romantic and platonic, personal and professional. So we took their advice and developed storylines that are really pertinent to these adults. They deal with issues that are relatable; for example, roommate troubles, finding a girlfriend or boyfriend, wanting a pet, hanging out with friends, dealing with health issues, and talking things out with a member of one's support staff. We included large scale black and white photos to add to the unique reading experience.

So that the stories would be accessible to the widest possible audience, we determined that we would keep them between a first and third grade reading level. We used two scoring systems to determine this: The Flesch-Kincaid System and The Fry Readability System. The Flesch-Kincaid Grade Level formula and the Flesch Reading Ease formula have been determined to be among the most reliable formulas for determining the difficulty of passages in English. The Fry Readability System is widely used to determine readability, especially in the healthcare industry. Using these two systems, which deliver grade level readability scores, allowed us to compare two scores for each story in order to gauge reliability. The short stories in this collection range from 1.5 to 3.5 on the Flesch-Kincaid scale and 2 to 4 on the Fry Readability scale. The stories in the book are arranged roughly in order of difficulty. Those with lower reading levels begin the book, and the more challenging stories are at the end.

Writing the stories presented some unexpected challenges. In order to keep the reading level low, we had to consider vocabulary, grammar, and literary style. We had frequent discussions on the use of figurative speech—how to keep the text fun to read and still easy to understand. When all was said and done, every phrase in these short stories was carefully considered with the goal of universal access.

The purpose of the questions at the end of each story is to encourage self-reflection as well as group discussion. They are not intended to be a quiz. Additionally, each story has a particular life lesson embedded within; however, we in no way wanted this to interfere with the fun and enjoyment of reading the story. Although some of the issues addressed in these stories are weighty, humor is interwoven and a defining characteristic of these stories.

Clearly, we wrote these short stories to be read within our book clubs. Yet, we believe access to these stories can benefit many people, including individuals with IDD and/or learning disabilities or challenges, people for whom English is a second language, and adults who are functionally illiterate. To that end, adults with disabilities, special educators, reading specialists, librarians, and book club coordinators will find this a wonderful book to add to their collection.

Finally, we hope that reading this collection of short stories will inspire people to seek fuller and richer literacy and lifelong learning experiences. We hope this is just the tip of the iceberg.

Bad Hair Day

Grace did not want to wake up. It was early in the morning, and very cold outside. It had snowed last night. She wanted to stay in bed.

Grace's alarm clock was ringing. She was too tired to turn it off so it kept ringing. Grace felt like throwing her alarm clock against the wall. She finally grabbed the clock and turned it off.

Grace lay still in her bed. She thought about how hard it would be to get to work with all that snow and cold weather outside. *Brrr.*

And now she had to think about taking a shower. *Brrr.* She did not want to shower. Grace knew how cold it would feel at first.

Maybe she would skip the shower. But she could not do that because she had not showered the day before. So she took a deep breath and hopped into the shower.

Grace's roommate, Beth, was still asleep. It was her day off, so she got to sleep late. Grace tried not to make noise while she ate breakfast. Sometimes she ate with her mouth open. Her dad would say Grace sounded like a cow when she ate.

Grace looked at the clock. It was time to go to her job at the library. But she had not brushed her hair yet. Grace knew her hair was messy, but she was out of time. She had to catch the bus.

What would her boss say about her hair? Her boss had talked to Grace about looking neat for work. What would her boyfriend, Alan, think? Would he still like her even with messy hair?

Grace was worried. But off she went to the bus stop anyway.

It was cold on the bus. Grace wore her hat and gloves. She wondered what her hair would look like after she took off her hat. Would it be even messier?

Grace had a hairbrush. Did she remember to bring it with her? Grace looked for the brush in her purse. She could not find it.

The bus got Grace to work on time. It was always on time. Joe was the bus driver. He was nice to Grace. Joe liked people. He also liked cats.

This morning Joe showed Grace a picture of his cat. His cat was named Meow. Grace thought Meow was cute. She also thought Meow's hair looked a lot neater than hers.

Grace had to walk three blocks to work after she got off the bus. There was a lot of snow on the sidewalk. Her feet were cold. She walked as fast as she could. Finally, she got to the library.

Grace was happy to be there. She had worked at the library for the last two years. Her job was to put away books and CDs when they were returned. Grace worked from 8:00 a.m. to 2:00 p.m., three days a week.

Her boyfriend, Alan, worked at the library too. His job was to do cleaning. He worked full-time. Alan and Grace had been dating for a few months. They had gone to school together when they were younger, but they were not boyfriend and girlfriend then.

Grace wanted to find a mirror. She wanted to see how bad her hair looked. She walked very fast to the bathroom.

Looking in the mirror, she saw that her hair was not *too* bad. But she still needed a brush. Maybe she could just use her hands to smooth it down and straighten it a little. No, she could not do that. It might make her hair look like a bowl of spaghetti.

Then what if Alan called her "Spaghetti Head"?

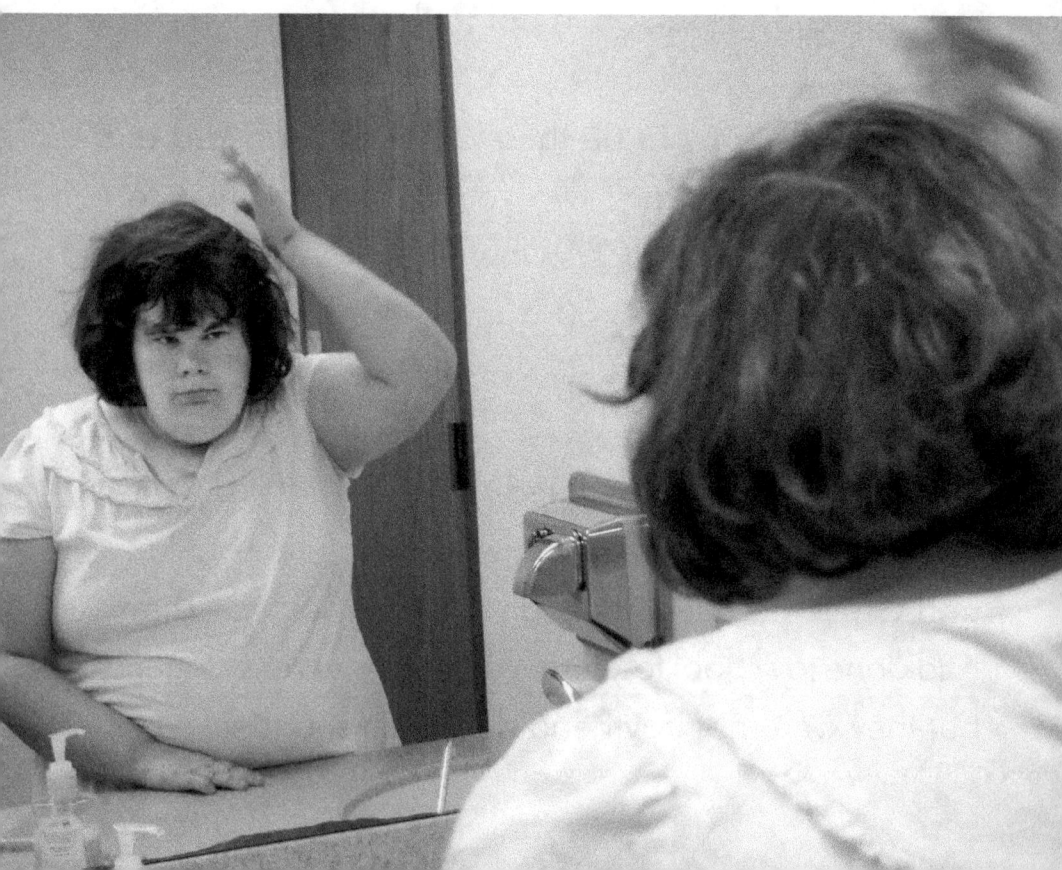

Or her boss told her to find another job because her hair was so messy? That would be the worst. Grace was becoming upset.

There were only six minutes left before Grace had to start work. She looked around the library for Alan. Maybe he would have a hairbrush. Or at least he could help her calm down.

She saw Alan at the end of the hall. He was happy to see Grace. She told him all about her bad hair day.

Alan thought she was being silly. He always thought Grace looked fantastic. He let Grace talk and did not say much so she would know he cared.

Alan told Grace he had a big comb in his locker. He would be happy to let her use it. Grace did not think a comb would work. Alan said he would help her and that her hair would look great.

There were four minutes left before Grace had to start work. So she asked Alan to go get his comb quickly.

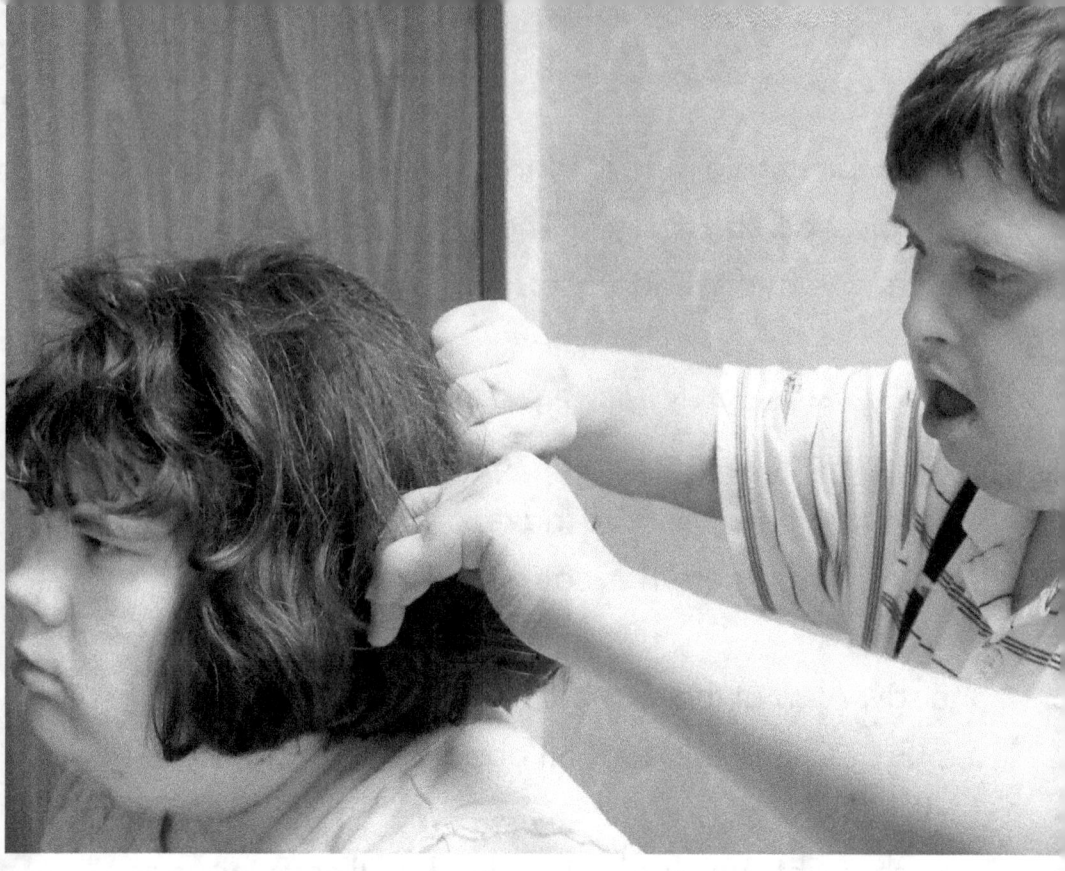

When Alan returned with the comb, Grace started combing, but there were a couple knots in the back of her head from wearing her hat. She could not reach them. Alan said she needed to trust him to do her hair.

Only Grace's mother had ever done her hair. No one else. But Grace had to trust Alan.

Grace was nervous. There was no mirror for her to see what Alan was doing. Alan began to comb. It hurt. Grace said, "Ouch, be careful!"

Alan felt bad. He said he was sorry. There were only three minutes left before Grace had to start work. Alan was trying his best. At last he was done.

"You look beautiful," Alan said. Grace touched her hair and said it felt good. She gave Alan a big hug and thanked him. Grace ran off to work.

Grace got to her desk right on time. Her boss, Ann, was there. They said good morning to each other. Grace was worried that Ann would say something about her hair. She was worried that Ann would think she did not look neat enough for work.

"It is really cold this morning," Ann said.

"Yes, it is," Grace agreed.

"Your hair looks pretty today, Grace," Ann said. Grace was surprised! She smiled and felt happy. Then Ann said, "I'm having a bad hair day."

"I thought *I* was having a bad hair day!" said Grace. "I think your hair looks nice, Ann."

"You think so? Thank you. I'd like to have thick, curly hair like yours," Ann said.

"Oh, thanks," Grace said. She thought about how upset she had been all morning. Now she was happy to get to work and stop thinking about her hair.

Grace had a wonderful day.

What Do You Think?

1. Grace had to get ready for work very fast. How do you feel if you have to hurry?

2. Why is it important to be on time for work?

3. Grace was very worried about the way her hair looked. Do you care about the way your hair looks when you go places?

4. How would you change your hair if you could?

How To Find a Girlfriend

Jake had a good life. He had graduated from high school and now he worked at a gym near his house. He really liked his job. But Jake had one problem. There was something Jake still wanted.

He really wanted a girlfriend. But he didn't know how to find one. How do you find a girlfriend? Jake thought about it. Then he had some ideas.

Jake joined a bowling group. He had always liked bowling, ever since he was little. When he was little, his favorite thing was getting a strike and seeing the screen light up and flash "Strike!" three times.

Now Jake hoped he might find a girlfriend in the bowling group. Every week he had a great time getting strikes and hanging out with his new friends. But none of the girls in the group were his age. So, he didn't find a girlfriend at bowling.

He decided to keep bowling anyway since he was having so much fun. But now how was Jake going to find a girlfriend?

Jake had a support person named Tim who took him places like shopping, doctor appointments, and the movies. Jake knew how to take the bus, but he couldn't drive. Tim could drive.

One day Tim invited Jake to go to a swing dancing class. It sounded fun.

Jake looked up the swing dance class on the Internet. It was at the YWCA. You had to pay five dollars for the class.

Jake and Tim went to the swing dancing class together. The teacher taught everyone how to dance. When the music played, each boy danced with the girl who was near him. When the music stopped, everyone moved and got a new dance partner.

Jake met lots of girls. He liked them. But he didn't find a girlfriend.

Jake thought of another idea.

Jake liked to help out in his community. He volunteered at the library where he helped put away DVDs that had been returned. He also helped out at a small store near his house that sold things from all over the world.

Everyone at this store was a volunteer. One volunteer told Jake about a community clean-up day at the local university. Jake decided he would go to the clean-up day. He could help his community and maybe find a girlfriend at the same time.

On the clean-up day, each volunteer got a plastic bag and plastic gloves. Everyone walked around and put trash in the plastic bags.

When the plastic bag was full, you brought it to the big trashcan and got a drink.

Jake filled up his plastic bag and went to get a drink. A girl was giving everyone the drinks. She smiled when she looked at Jake. Then she asked, "Do you want a drink?"

"Sure," Jake said. She gave him a drink. It was lemonade. He finished it and asked, "Could I have another lemonade, please?"

"Of course," she said.

"What is your name?" Jake asked.

"I'm Maya," she said.

"I'm Jake," he told her. Then Jake got another empty plastic bag and went to pick up more trash.

When he brought back the bag full of trash, Maya was still at the drink table. Jake said, "Hi Maya. Could I have another drink, please?"

She said, "Sure." Jake and Maya started to talk. First they talked about the weather. Then they talked about how nice the university looked without trash on the ground.

Jake asked, "What do you like to do, Maya?"

Maya said, "I like to go to the movies. What do you like to do?"

"I like to go to the movies, too. I also like to go bowling," Jake said.

"What kind of movies do you like?" Maya asked.

Jake said, "I like comedies."

Maya smiled and said, "I like comedies, too!"

Jake thought Maya was pretty. He liked talking to her. So Jake had another idea.

"Would you like to go to a movie with me?" Jake asked.

"Sure," Maya said. Then she smiled again.

Jake said, "I will look on the Internet and find a good movie. Do you have an email address or should I call you on the phone?"

Maya said, "You can call me." Maya wrote her phone number on a piece of paper and gave it to Jake.

The next day, Jake found a good movie on the Internet that was playing in a nearby theater. He called Maya.

"Hello," said a woman's voice on the phone.

"Hi, may I talk to Maya, please?" Jake asked.

"This is Maya. Hi, is this Jake?" Maya asked.

"Yes, it is. I found a funny movie I think we will both like. Would you like to see it with me tonight?"

"Okay," Maya said. "That sounds like fun."

At the movie, Maya had popcorn and Jake had candy. When Maya finished her popcorn, she wiped the butter off her hands. Then she reached over and held Jake's hand. Jake felt very happy.

Jake and Maya lived close to each other. One night, Jake walked to Maya's house and they had dinner together. A few nights later, Jake and Maya went to another movie together.

On another day, they met at the park and went for a walk together. While they were walking, Jake asked Maya if she would like to try bowling. Maya said, "Sure."

Maya tried bowling. She was not a good bowler. She got lots of gutter balls.

Jake felt bad for Maya. "I'm sorry this isn't very fun for you," he said.

"It *is* fun! I'm not very good at bowling, but I am still having fun. I have fun being with you," Maya said.

Then Jake had a very good idea. He sat down next to Maya and looked in her eyes. "Would you be my girlfriend?" Jake asked.

"Yes!" Maya said.

They grinned at each other. Then Maya stood up and threw another gutter ball. She giggled and Jake laughed back.

They held hands all the way home from the bowling alley. "So, this is how it feels to have a girlfriend!" Jake said.

"How does it feel?" Maya asked.

"Awesome!" said Jake.

What Do You Think?

1. How did Jake meet Maya?

2. Have you ever had a boyfriend or girlfriend? Where did you meet?

3. When Jake was looking for a girlfriend, he tried to meet people at different activities like bowling and swing dancing. Where can you meet new people?

4. What is the best part of having a boyfriend or girlfriend?

5. Where would you like to go on a date?

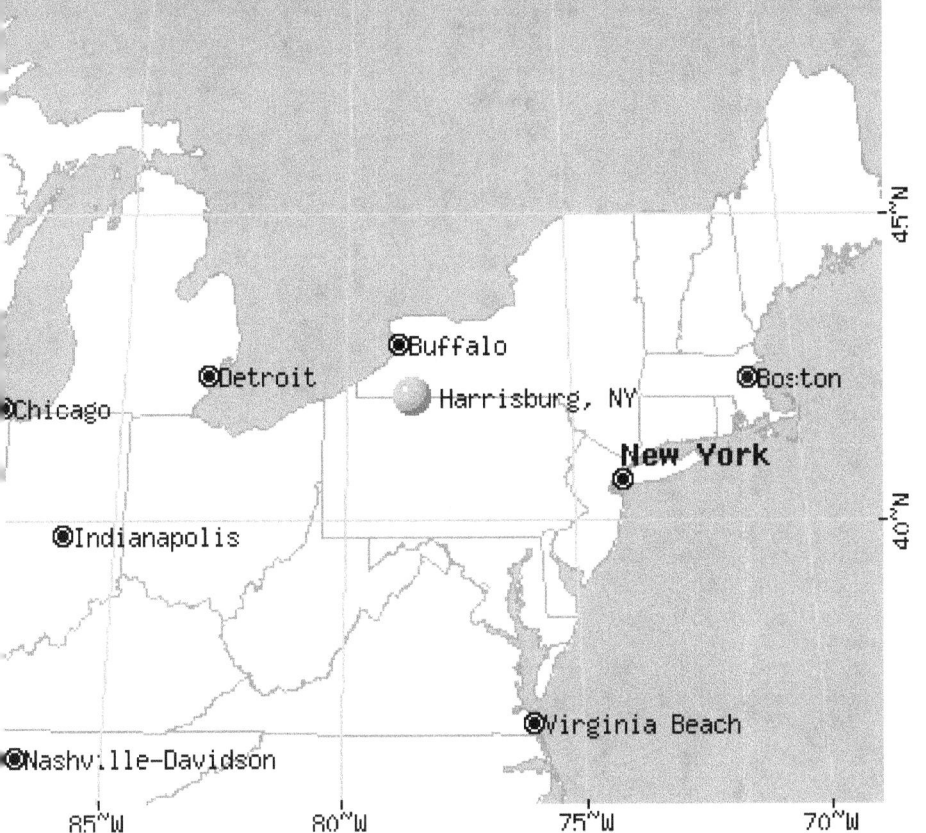

Road Trip

My cousin Damon and I are good friends. Damon is 21 and I am 22. Last month, Damon and I went on a road trip to visit friends in New York City. We live four hours away from New York City.

We planned to go to the Empire State Building and Central Park. We were excited to explore the whole "Big Apple." Some people call New York City the "Big Apple" but I don't know why.

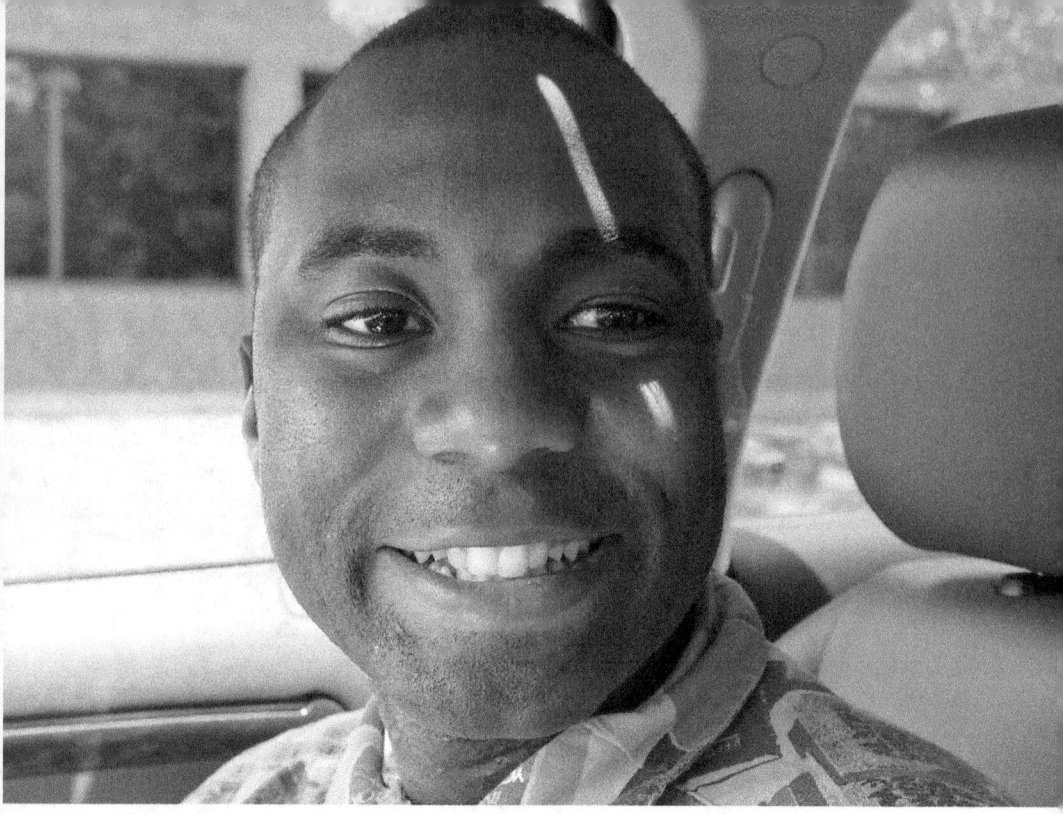

Damon drove because he likes to be in charge. He thinks he is a better driver than I am. He thinks he is a better driver than *everyone*.

I was more interested in the music we would listen to on our road trip. I picked out all of the songs and put them on my iPod. Damon and I both agreed that I did a very good job.

"Nice job with the music, Marcus," Damon said.

"What?" I said. I couldn't hear him because the music was too loud. Damon turned the music down.

"Sweet music," Damon said. "Man, this weekend is going to be awesome."

"I know! I can't wait to get there," I said. "Oh, you're going to love this song," I said. I started a new song that was all about New York City.

"Nice!" Damon said. Both of us smiled.

The only problem was that I had a headache. I was trying to ignore it. But it wouldn't go away.

We stopped at a gas station so I could get a bottle of water. My mom says sometimes people get headaches just because they need to drink more water. But the water tasted funny and I was starting to feel dizzy.

"Hey, buddy, get in your own lane!" Damon yelled at another driver.

"Could you stop yelling so much? It is so annoying," I said. "And maybe we could turn the music down. It's too loud."

"Man, Marcus, you are cranky today," Damon said.

"Me? You are the one who is always cranky! You are cranky and loud," I said.

"Geez, maybe you should try to take a nap or something," Damon said as he changed lanes.

"Fine," I said. I laid the seat back and closed my eyes. I felt weird, like I might get sick. I heard Damon call my name. I don't know what happened after that.

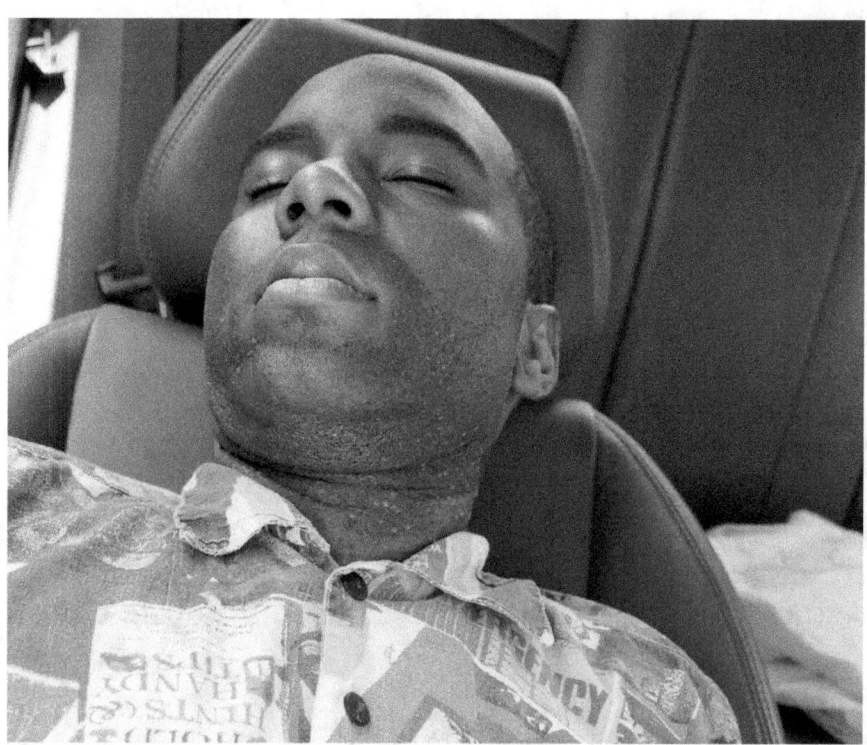

The next thing I remember was Damon holding my arm tight. The car was stopped.

"Marcus! Hey, man! Marcus!" he said loudly. He sounded very upset. Why was he squeezing my arm so tight? Why was he yelling my name?

"Wait, I think he stopped shaking. Marcus! Are you okay? No, he didn't answer me. What should I do now?" Damon said.

I was confused. Then I figured out that he was talking to somebody else on his cell phone. Suddenly, I saw bright lights, like lights from an ambulance.

"Okay, they are here! Bye," Damon said. I heard him open his car door. "Should I stay in the car?" he asked someone.

"Yes, that is fine for now," said a woman. Then the woman opened the car door by me. It was hard to look at her. Everything looked bright and fuzzy.

"Sir? How are you?" Now her hand was on my arm. "What is his name?"

"Marcus," Damon answered.

"Marcus, can you talk to me?" she asked.

I could see more clearly now. I saw that she was wearing a uniform with a name tag. I saw the letters EMT. I remembered EMT stood for Emergency Medical Technician. These are people who help in emergencies.

I got very upset and confused. All I could say was, "Um."

I heard the woman tell Damon that they would need to take me to the hospital. I got more scared and started to breathe fast. "It's okay, you just need to stay calm," she said to me.

"Hey man, you are going to be okay. I'm with you. You are going to be okay," Damon said to me. I felt a little better when I heard Damon talking to me.

Then I felt like I could talk. I asked, "Damon, what happened?"

"Right after you tried to take a nap, you just started shaking. I pulled the car over to the side of the road and called 911. The ambulance is here now," Damon told me. I could tell he was upset, too.

"How long was I shaking?" I asked.

"It felt like a long time, but it was probably about three minutes," Damon said. Then he asked the EMT, "What do you think happened?"

"It sounds like he had a seizure. It was good he was already lying down in a soft place," she told Damon.

"Marcus, have you ever had a seizure before?" she asked me.

"No. Why did this happen?" I asked. I could feel tears in my eyes.

"Right now we don't know. We are going to take you to the hospital and make sure you are okay," she said.

A man in an EMT uniform walked up next to the woman. "Hi buddy," he said to me. "We're going to lay you on this stretcher so we can put you in the back of the ambulance." I got nervous again.

"It is okay, Marcus. A stretcher is just a bed on wheels," the woman said. "By the way, my name is Carla. This is my co-worker Todd."

"Should I go with you?" asked Damon. Carla asked Damon if he felt okay to drive.

"Yes, I'm fine," Damon answered.

Carla said, "Okay. It would be best to get your car off the highway. You can follow us to the hospital."

As Carla and Todd put me in the ambulance, I saw Damon looking at me. He looked scared. Then he waved at me.

"Damon, I'm sorry, man. This is no good. I'm sorry," I said.

"Hey man, don't say you are sorry. I'm just glad you are okay," Damon said. I nodded my head.

The ride to the hospital was short and bumpy. The lights in the back of the ambulance were bright. Then I thought about something and reached for the phone in my pocket.

"I should call my mom," I said.

"Damon said he was going to call your mom for you," Carla said.

"Oh, okay. Oh man, she is going to flip out. Poor Damon," I said. I felt like laughing, but I was so tired and my stomach was still upset.

"Yes, parents usually get upset when their child is sick," said Carla.

"Well, my mom makes a big deal of everything. She's going to freak out on Damon. I mean, really freak out," I said.

When we got to the hospital, some nurses rolled me into a room that had curtains instead of walls. The EMTs, Carla and Todd, talked to the nurses. Then Carla walked over to me and said, "You take care, Marcus."

"Thank you," I said. Carla and Todd waved goodbye and walked out of the room. A doctor walked in and started talking to the nurses, but no one looked at me.

It makes me nervous when people talk about me, like I can't hear them. I wished they would look at me and talk to me. Then everyone left the room except one nurse.

"Excuse me," I said. "Where am I?"

"You are in a hospital," said one of the nurses.

"Yes, I know. I mean, what town are we in? My cousin and I left home in Harrisburg and we were driving to New York City when...when this happened," I told her.

"I see. You are in Hamburg, Pennsylvania. You must have been driving for about an hour. My name is Rachel. Dr. Gibbs will be in to talk with you soon. Right now we are going to do some blood tests to find out why you had a seizure. Are you afraid of needles?" Rachel asked.

"No," I said.

"Good. Do you have any health problems?" she asked.

"A few months ago I found out I have diabetes. Do you think that could have caused this?" I asked.

"Maybe," she answered. "Diabetes means that your body has trouble keeping the right amount of sugar in your blood. If your blood does not have the right amount of sugar, it can cause a lot of problems.

"Sometimes if your blood sugar is too low, it can cause seizures. The blood tests will help us know for certain what happened," Rachel said. Then she asked, "Can you tell me what you ate today?"

I couldn't remember eating anything. I was too excited about going to New York to think about food. "I guess I haven't had anything to eat today," I said.

"Well, it is four o'clock in the afternoon. That is a long time for anyone to go without food. For someone with diabetes, that can be dangerous," she said. "How are you feeling right now?"

"Woozy and tired," I answered.

Damon walked into the room. Rachel turned around and said hello. Then she asked him if he was a member of my family.

"Yes, I'm his cousin. Is it okay if I'm in here?" asked Damon.

Rachel smiled and looked at me. She said, "That is up to Marcus."

I nodded my head.

"Okay. I'm going to get a few things and I will be right back," Rachel said. She left the room and Damon walked over to me. I reached out my hand, and Damon grabbed my hand with his.

"Hey, man. Are you alright?" Damon asked.

"I guess so. They are going to do some tests. But it seems like the seizure has something to do with my diabetes. I'm sorry, man. I ruined our road trip to New York," I said.

Damon shook his head and looked at me. "Marcus, you didn't ruin anything. We can go to New York another time. You don't need to be sorry. I'm just glad you are okay," he said.

Then he added, "I don't know how well your mom is doing, though."

I groaned and laughed a little. "Did she flip out? Is she coming here?" I asked.

"Yes, she flipped out," Damon said with a smile. "And yes, she and your dad and your sister are on their way here."

"Thanks for calling," I said.

"No big deal," he said. "I called the guys in New York, too. They said they are sorry you got sick. They want you to feel better soon so we can plan another visit."

"Thanks," I said. I felt so tired. Damon said he was going to go see if he could find a place to buy a cup of coffee.

A minute later, the nurse, Rachel, came back and took some blood. When she left, it was quiet.

Then I heard the sound of someone crying on the other side of the curtain. I realized it was Damon crying. He was talking to his mom.

"Mom, it was scary. He wouldn't stop shaking," Damon said. He sniffed and kept crying. I felt bad that I had scared Damon.

I thought about how I would feel if I saw Damon have a seizure. I would be scared too.

When he came back in the room, he pretended like he wasn't crying. I didn't mention it. I just told him that I was glad he was there with me.

Damon nodded and said, "I wouldn't know what to do without you, man."

"I know what you mean," I said to Damon. He sat down in the chair by my bed and took a deep breath. We were both tired. Soon, I fell asleep.

I woke up when my family walked into the room. They hugged me and Damon a lot. Everyone thanked Damon for making sure I was safe.

I could see that my mom had been crying, but she was much calmer than I thought she would be. She just sat on the bed next to me and held my hand. My dad said she prayed the whole way to the hospital.

Dr. Gibbs walked into the room. "Hello," he said. "Marcus, is this your family?" I nodded. "Is it okay if I talk about your test results in front of them?"

"Yes," I said.

Dr. Gibbs looked at me and said, "I believe your seizure was caused by low blood sugar." He explained that my blood sugar was so low that it made my brain send too many messages to the rest of my body. That was why I could not stop shaking.

But he had good news. I could stop this from happening again by checking my blood sugar and eating regularly.

On the drive home, my family and I had a long talk about my health. I realized it is my job to take care of my body. If I don't, I could have another seizure.

So now I make sure I eat as often as I need to. I also eat healthy food instead of all the sweets I used to eat.

My family, including Damon, learned what to do in case I have another seizure.

I hope that doesn't happen again, but it is nice to know that someone will be able to help me if it does.

Damon and I have planned another road trip to New York City for next weekend. I am going to bring plenty of healthy snacks to eat along the way.

We are both excited to finally explore New York City. I'm going to find out why they call it "The Big Apple."

What Do You Think?

1. If you could go to New York City, what would you like to do there?

2. Have you ever gone on a long trip away from home? Did you go in a car or airplane? Where did you go?

3. Have you ever had a seizure? Or have you ever seen someone have a seizure? How did it make you feel?

4. What did Marcus say he should do so he does not have another seizure?

Slugger

"Where did my hat go?" George asked his friend Doug. George had been looking for his favorite hat. He thought his housemate Doug was playing a trick on him by hiding his hat. Doug liked to joke around a lot.

They were getting ready to go outside to play baseball. George could not play baseball without his hat. It was his lucky hat!

Doug said, "I don't know where your hat is, George. Did you leave it under your bed again?" They were in George's bedroom. So George looked quickly under his bed.

"It's not there. I know you hid my hat. How about... if you give me my hat I will give you some ice cream," George said. Doug loved ice cream. The two friends ate ice cream together almost every day.

"Ice cream sounds great! But I don't have your hat," Doug said.

"Give me my hat, Doug!" George said. He was angry.

"I don't have your hat! Honest!" Doug said. Their other housemate Mandy heard the shouting and walked into George's room. Doug asked Mandy, "Have you seen George's hat?"

She said, "No. Let's go, George. Forget about your hat. It's time to play baseball." Mandy wanted to play baseball right away. Sometimes Mandy could be impatient.

George said, "You know I can't play baseball without my hat." He flipped over his pillow. But his hat was not there.

He folded his arms. Today was turning out to be a bad day. He did not feel like playing baseball anymore.

Mandy said, "Stop being grumpy, George! You are acting like a child."

George did not care. He sat on his bed. He felt like crying. Why weren't they helping him find his hat?

Doug tried to make a joke, "Knock, knock."

"Knock it off!" yelled George. He hit his pillow.

Mandy gave George a mean look. "Geez!" she said. She grabbed George's backpack and looked through it. The hat was not there. Doug took another look under George's bed, but the hat was not there.

George was getting more upset. He had lost his favorite hat. It had been his favorite hat for a long time.

George had bought it over ten years ago when he went to a football game. It was black and white and had red letters on it.

The more he thought about his lost hat, the more he felt like hitting his pillow again.

Doug sat down beside George. He bumped George's knee with his own knee and said, "George, let's go play baseball. You will feel better once you get outside.

"And maybe your hat is on the baseball field. It's not in here. We know that much."

George grumbled. He did not want to speak. But Doug was right. They might find the hat somewhere else. So George, Doug, and Mandy walked down to the baseball field.

There were other people playing at the field, and they were happy to see George. They said, "Oh! It's George, the Slugger! Come join my team!"

George still did not want to talk to anyone. He sat on the bench and waited for his turn to hit the ball. He was still trying to think about where he could have left his hat.

He had washed it a couple days ago, but he had worn it since then. Just yesterday morning, a new co-worker had told George that he liked his hat.

George was starting to wonder if someone had stolen his hat. Now he was really mad!

When it was George's turn at bat, he stepped up to the plate and swung at the ball with all his strength.

"Strike!" shouted the umpire.

George grunted. He wasn't used to getting strikes.

The pitcher threw the ball again.

"Strike two!" the umpire shouted.

George was really frustrated now. First he lost his hat. Now he was about to strike out.

George thought to himself, "I'm going to strike out because I don't have my lucky hat. Could this day get any worse?"

The pitcher threw the ball a third time. Bam! This time George hit the ball. The bat made a loud cracking noise when it struck the ball. The ball went flying all the way across the fence. It was a home run!

"Wow! Great hit, George!" Doug shouted.

George ran around the bases while Mandy ran around the fence to get the ball. George heard his friends cheering him on as he ran. He felt great. After he crossed home plate, he gave Doug a high-five.

"You didn't need your lucky hat after all!" Doug said.

George had forgotten about his lost hat until Doug said that. "Why did you have to remind me about my hat?" he asked Doug. He walked over to the bench and sat down. Now he was grumpy again.

Doug followed him. "George, you just got a home run without your hat! You don't need a lucky hat.

But we can keep looking for it after the game if you want to," he said. Doug was a very kind friend, even if he did like to play tricks on people.

George looked up and noticed Mandy walking toward him. She had gone to get his home run ball on the other side of the fence. Her hands were behind her back and she looked like she was about to laugh.

"I have a present for you, George," Mandy said. Then she handed George his lucky hat.

"My hat!" George exclaimed. "Where did you find it?"

"It was near the ball on the other side of the fence. How did it get there?" Mandy was curious.

George remembered now. Last night during baseball practice, a teammate had hit a home run. George walked behind the fence to find the ball. As he was looking, a bumblebee began buzzing around him. It wouldn't leave him alone.

"I took off my hat to swat at the bee. But it didn't help. The bee kept chasing me! I must have dropped my hat when I was running away from the bee!" George said.

"Thanks for finding my hat, Mandy," George said. He was smiling now.

"You're welcome. I'm glad I didn't find the bumblebee!" Mandy said.

Doug gave George a pat on the back. "We're glad to see you smile, Slugger," he said.

George was glad he went out to play baseball with friends instead of staying inside and hitting his pillow. It was much more fun to hit the baseball.

What Do You Think?

1. Do you have a favorite hat, favorite shirt, or anything that you think is lucky?

2. How did George feel when he could not find his lucky hat?

3. Do you have housemates like George does? Do they help you out when you are having a bad day?

4. George and his housemates do fun things together like play baseball and eat ice cream. What kinds of things do you do with your friends?

5. What is your favorite kind of ice cream?

Doctor Visit

Harry had been having pain in his ear for about one week. The pain was getting worse. Harry was worried. He decided to talk to Steve about it.

Steve helped Harry with things around the house and drove him places he needed to go. Harry trusted Steve.

Steve told Harry that he needed to go to the doctor. Harry didn't have a regular doctor. And Harry did not want to go to any old doctor. Steve helped Harry call and make an appointment anyway. Steve said it was important.

Harry trusted Steve but he was still afraid. Harry did not like doctors. He did not think they were nice to him.

Harry felt nervous in waiting rooms. He thought people looked at him funny. It always took a long time to see the doctor. And it was always cold in the doctor's office.

But Harry did like nurses. He thought they were pretty. It was easy for Harry to talk to nurses.

Because doctors made him nervous, Harry asked Steve to take him to his appointment. But when Steve came to pick him up, Harry said his ear felt better.

Steve did not believe him. He knew Harry did not want to see the doctor.

"Don't worry, Harry," Steve said. "Dr. Palmer is my dad's doctor. Dr. Palmer is very nice." Steve said that Dr. Palmer would help Harry feel better.

Harry and Steve left to go see the doctor. They drove in Steve's car. It was small and blue and had lots of bumper stickers on it.

Harry was nervous. Steve turned on the radio. He played country music. Harry liked country music.

"Will we have to wait a long time to see the doctor?" Harry asked. Steve said he did not know. "Will the doctor give me medicine?" Harry asked.

"Maybe," said Steve. Harry pressed his hand against his painful ear. "Try to relax, Harry," Steve said.

"I am trying," Harry said. "But my ear really hurts."

Steve told Harry a joke. "What do you call a dog that cannot bark?" Steve asked.

"I don't know," Harry said.

"A hush puppy," Steve said.

"Very funny," Harry said. Harry tried to laugh, but his ear hurt too much. They arrived at the doctor's office fifteen minutes later.

Dr. Palmer had a big waiting room. There was a large fish tank and a lot of magazines. There were pictures of mountains, fields, and trees on the walls.

Steve was parking the car. Harry looked at the fish tank, and then he went to the front desk to check in.

The lady behind the desk asked, "What is your name, sir?" She had a big smile and red hair. She made Harry feel better.

"Welcome, Harry," she said. "Because you are here for the first time, we have some forms for you to fill out." She told Harry she would help him if he had any questions.

Harry looked at all the papers and questions. They made him nervous. He was glad Steve would be in soon to help him.

Steve had been helping Harry do more things on his own. Harry knew Steve would be proud if he started to fill out the forms on his own.

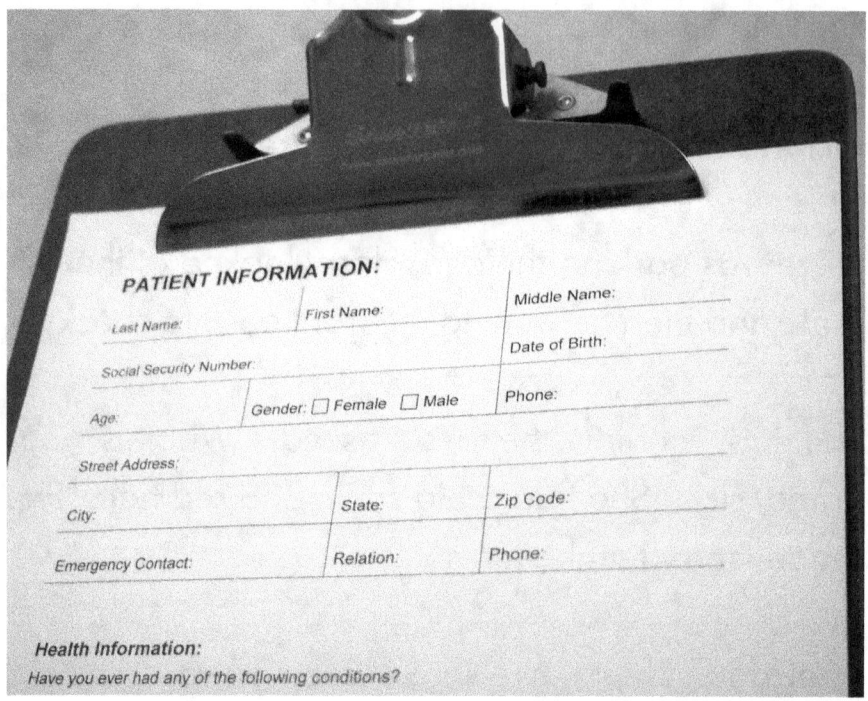

PATIENT INFORMATION:

Last Name:

First Name:

Middle Name:

Social Security Number:

Date of Birth:

Age:

Gender: ☐ Female ☐ Male

Phone:

Street Address:

City:

State:

Zip Code:

Emergency Contact:

Relation:

Phone:

Health Information:

Have you ever had any of the following conditions?

Harry was surprised at how many of the questions he was able to answer on his own! When Steve came in, Harry was almost finished. Steve only helped with a few questions. Harry gave the forms back to the nice lady behind the desk.

There were other people in the waiting room. Some of them looked sick and some did not. There were two children playing at a small table. They were putting together a puzzle. Harry did not like puzzles. They made his eyes hurt.

Harry was cold. This doctor's office was cold like the other doctors' offices. Harry felt nervous.

"Harry?" a nurse called. She said hello to Harry and Steve. She told Steve they would call him if they had any questions. Steve told Harry everything would be fine.

Harry nodded and followed the nurse through the door and down the hallway. "My name is Vicky. How are you feeling today, Harry?" she asked.

"Fine," said Harry. He did not feel fine. But he did not feel like talking, either.

Vicky smiled at Harry and asked him to step on a scale. Vicky wrote down Harry's weight. Then she took his blood pressure, and wrote that down too.

"Okay, Harry, follow me please," Vicky said. They walked around the corner and into a very bright room with two chairs. "Hop up on this table. Would you like to look at a magazine while you wait for Dr. Palmer?" Vicky asked.

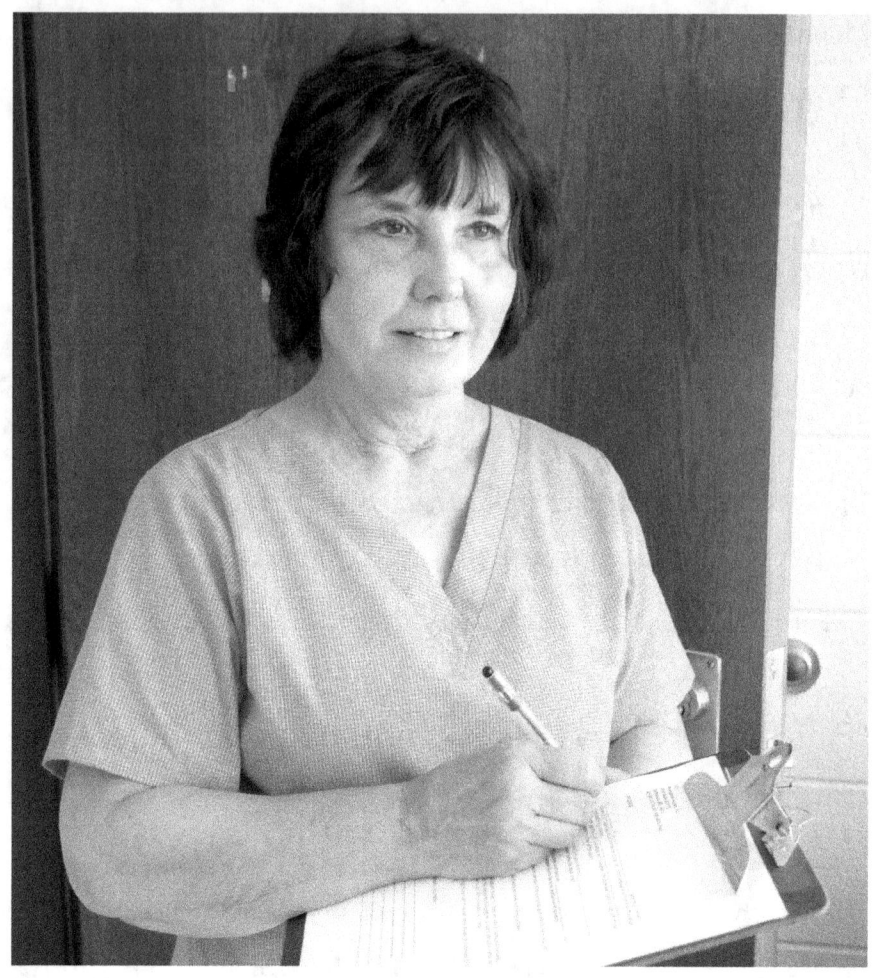

More waiting. Waiting made Harry feel more nervous. "No, thank you," Harry said. Then he asked, "How long do I have to wait?"

"Not too long," Vicky said, and then she left the room. Harry tried to relax. Steve said Dr. Palmer was nice. Harry did not need to worry.

Harry's ear hurt and his stomach was beginning to hurt too. He wanted to go home. He thought about his room. He felt safe there. Harry was thinking about his own fish tank when someone knocked on the door.

"Hello?" said Harry. He was startled.

"May I come in?" asked a woman's voice. Harry said yes and then wondered why he had to see another nurse before seeing Dr. Palmer. This was taking a long time.

The woman walked in and put her hand out to shake Harry's hand. "Hi Harry, I'm Dr. Palmer," she said.

"Hi," said Harry. Harry was confused. He thought Dr. Palmer was a man. Every doctor he had ever seen was a man. Harry said, "You are Dr. Palmer? I thought you were going to be a man."

Dr. Palmer laughed. "Well, I'm Dr. Karen Palmer. It's nice to meet you. Let's talk about why you are here today," she said.

"Um, my ear hurts," Harry said. Dr. Palmer asked Harry to show her where it hurt.

Dr. Palmer asked Harry a few more questions and then asked if she could put something called an "otoscope" into his ear and take a closer look. She showed Harry the otoscope. Harry thought it looked like a very small flashlight. Harry said that would be okay.

Dr. Palmer was very gentle and moved slowly. It felt a little funny but it didn't hurt. Harry decided that Steve was right. Dr. Palmer *was* very kind.

Then Dr. Palmer said, "I believe I know what is wrong with you, Harry. You have an infection in your ear."

"Uh oh," Harry said. He was worried.

Dr. Palmer explained that ear infections can be very painful but usually aren't too serious. Harry would need to take some medicine to help kill the infection.

"Okay," said Harry, quietly. "Will it stop hurting then?"

"In a week or so, when the medicine has cleared up the infection, your ear will stop hurting. We can help you feel better in the meantime by giving you medicine to relieve the pain," Dr. Palmer explained.

Harry was beginning to feel a bit confused. Was he supposed to take two different medicines? He asked, "Can Steve come in now?"

"Yes, of course," Dr. Palmer said. She opened the door, called to Vicky, and asked her to go get Steve. Harry was glad to see Steve when he walked into the room a minute later.

"Hey, Harry, how's your ear?" Steve asked. He patted Harry on the shoulder. Harry looked at Steve. Then he looked at Dr. Palmer. Then he looked back at Steve.

"It hurts. I have an infection. And I need to take medicine," Harry blurted out.

"Oh, Harry. I'm sorry. But don't worry. I'll help with the medicine and I'm sure your roommates will help cheer you up when you get home," said Steve.

A week later, Harry and Steve went back to Dr. Palmer's office for a follow-up appointment. Vicky was there again and this time Harry didn't think the waiting room felt as cold.

"I want Dr. Palmer to be my regular doctor," Harry said to Steve.

"Good choice, Harry," Steve said.

Soon Vicky brought Harry back to see the doctor. When Dr. Palmer came in the room, she was just as friendly as before. Harry felt very confident. He was sure of his decision to make Dr. Palmer his doctor. It felt good to make that decision all on his own.

This time, when Dr. Palmer looked inside Harry's ear with the otoscope, instead of feeling worried, Harry asked, "Hey, Dr. Palmer...What do you call a dog that can't bark?"

What Do You Think?

1. Who is your favorite doctor? Why do you like him or her?

2. Would you rather go to the doctor or to the dentist?

3. Harry had to take medicine for his ear infection. Have you ever had to take medication? How did you remember to take the medicine? Did someone help you?

4. What kinds of things do you need to do to stay healthy?

Evening Walks

Scott and his sister Helen were putting on their sneakers. It was time for their evening walk. Scott and Helen looked forward to their after-dinner walks through their neighborhood.

There was so much to do and see near their apartment. The library was across the street.

And it seemed like there was a shop or restaurant everywhere you looked. Scott was glad that he lived close enough to walk to all of these places.

When he lived with his parents, they had to drive everywhere. When Scott's parents died, he went to live with his sister, Helen. He missed his mother and father very much. But he was happy in his new home.

Helen said the walks were good for their health. "Our backsides are spreading!" Helen joked. "That means our bottoms are getting bigger. We need more exercise," she explained.

Scott and Helen liked their jobs. But neither job made them move around very much.

Helen repaired jewelry for a local jewelry store. Scott collected tickets from customers at the movie theater. He tore them in half and told the customers to enjoy their movie. When he could, he liked to do this while sitting on a stool.

On one of Scott and Helen's evening walks, they noticed a man sitting against the wall of the bank.

He was holding a cardboard sign. He looked like he hadn't had a bath in a long time. As they walked past him, Helen took a dollar out of her pocket and handed it to the man.

"Why did you give that man money?" Scott asked. "What did the sign say?"

"It said 'Homeless. Please help,'" Helen told Scott. "He needs money, so I gave him a dollar."

Scott didn't say anything.

"Do you know what it means to be homeless?" Helen asked.

Scott shook his head, so Helen explained. "Someone who is homeless doesn't have a place to live. We live in an apartment that keeps us warm in the winter and cool in the summer. A homeless person lives outside most of the time.

"I think it would be very hard to be homeless," Helen said.

"Why would somebody be homeless?" Scott asked.

"Well, there are many reasons why someone might be homeless. Sometimes people are homeless because they can't find a job, so they don't have enough money to pay rent. Some people are homeless because they have problems that make it hard for them to keep their jobs."

"He smelled bad. Why did you give him money?" Scott asked again.

"If you didn't get to shower very often, you would smell bad, too. In fact..." Helen sniffed in Scott's direction. Then she plugged her nose and waved her hand in front of her face, pretending that Scott smelled bad.

"Ha, ha, Helen," Scott said with a smile on his face. Scott and Helen liked to tease each other.

"I gave him a dollar because I think he needs it more than I do. It's a small thing I can do to help. People can also be helpful to the homeless by giving blankets, coats, water, and food."

"Oh. Can we bring him dinner tomorrow?" Scott asked.

"I suppose we could...if he's there again tomorrow night," Helen replied.

The next night, the man was there. Scott thought he looked very tired. They gave him a bag with a container of chili, a piece of bread, an apple, a bottle of water, and a spoon. When the man looked inside, Helen said, "I hope you like chili! It's our mother's famous recipe."

The man said, "Yes, thank you. Thank you." He was so quiet that Scott could hardly hear him. But he thought he saw a smile under the man's bushy beard.

Helen and Scott finished their walk quietly. They were both thinking about the homeless man.

They thought about what it would be like to have no home and no dinner.

Scott and Helen began to bring the man dinner a couple times each week. Helen would also give him a dollar from time to time. Scott thought that was nice of his sister, but he wasn't comfortable giving away any of his money or stuff. Helen said she understood.

One night Helen said to the man, "My name is Helen. This is my brother Scott."

"Hi, Scott and Helen. My name is Richard," said the man. "Thank you for helping me."

"You're welcome," Scott and Helen said at the same time.

"Why are you homeless?" asked Scott.

"Scott, that's none of our business," Helen said. But Richard answered anyway.

"Well, I moved here from Texas for my job. A couple weeks later, they laid me off. I spent a few months looking for another job, but I couldn't find one. I got behind on my rent, and they evicted me," he said.

Scott looked at Helen. He didn't know what it meant to be laid off and evicted. Helen said, "He lost his job and his landlord made him move out of his apartment because he did not have enough money to pay the rent bill."

"I wouldn't like it if that happened to me!" Scott said.

"No, it's no fun, that's for sure," said Richard.

"Why do you sit here?" Scott asked. Helen was afraid that Scott was asking too many questions, but Richard didn't seem to mind.

"Oh, this is a nice spot. I have these bushes to block the wind. The best part is the brick wall. The sun heats it up all day and it stays warm for a long time after the sun goes down," Richard answered.

"Oh," Scott and Helen said at the same time.

"Well, thank you again for your help. Last night's chicken and rice was very tasty." Scott thought he was smiling again, but it was hard to tell because Richard had such a thick beard.

A couple weeks later, Scott and Helen were on their usual evening walk. They went into the library to return a DVD. They walked past one of their favorite Chinese restaurants. Then they turned the corner by the bank where Richard sat.

Standing near Richard was a group of teenage boys and girls. They were laughing. As Scott and Helen got closer, they heard some of the things the boys and girls were saying.

One boy said, "Ever heard of a job?" The group laughed.

A girl said, "Or a shower?" The group laughed even harder.

Helen and Scott were furious. As Helen and Scott reached the group, they saw Richard looking down at the sidewalk.

"Stop! Stop it right now!" Helen yelled at the teens. "Why are you so hateful? Where are your parents? I should tell them what you're doing!"

The boys and girls just kept laughing. Now they were making fun of Helen too. Scott stared at the boys and girls and said, "Don't make fun of my sister. And don't make fun of my friend, Richard. That is mean!" Scott could feel tears in his eyes.

A boy said, "Come on, let's leave these losers alone." The group walked away.

"I am not a loser. YOU are the losers!" Scott yelled at them.

Helen put her hand on Scott's shoulder. She told him that it would be best to let the kids walk away. Then she walked over to Richard and sat down next to him. Scott followed and sat next to Helen.

"Oh, Richard, I'm so sorry. Those kids...those brats!" Now Helen felt tears in her eyes.

"It's no big thing. It happens," Richard said. "I ignore them and eventually they go away. But thanks for sticking up for me."

"It's just awful. They don't even know you!" Helen said.

"No, they don't. But I don't think I'd like to know them either," Richard said.

"Me neither!" Scott and Helen said at the same time.

"You two seem to do that a lot…say the same thing at the same time," said Richard.

"We know," Scott and Helen said, again at the same time.

Everyone laughed. They sat together against the warm brick wall for a long time. At one point, Helen said, "This is a good spot for people watching."

"Yes, I suppose it is," Richard said.

As the sun set, Helen stood up and said it was time for Scott and her to walk home. One more time she said, "I'm sorry, Richard."

He didn't say anything. He just waved his hand, like it was no big deal, like he was swatting away a fly. Scott and Helen began to walk away.

Then Scott had an idea. He reached into his pocket and pulled out a candy bar that he had planned to have as a treat after their walk.

"Here, Richard. This is for you," Scott said. It was the first time he had ever given anything of his own away, and he was surprised by how good it felt.

"Thank you, Scott," Richard said. This time, Scott was sure he saw Richard smile beneath his beard.

Later that night, Helen and Scott talked more about what happened. They both agreed that Richard didn't deserve to be treated so badly by those kids. They also agreed that sharing and helping out felt great. They wanted to do more.

The following week, Scott and Helen began volunteering at a local homeless shelter. Instead of just making food for Richard, they would help cook and serve meals once a week for many of the homeless people in their neighborhood.

Every once in a while their friend Richard came in for a meal. On those days, they enjoyed sitting and chatting with him like old times.

What Do You Think?

1. What do you think it would be like to be homeless?

2. Sometimes people say, "It is better to give than receive." What do you think that means?

3. How do you feel when you help someone?

4. Helen and Scott go on walks through their neighborhood each night. They live in a busy neighborhood with shops and restaurants. What is your neighborhood like?

Adventures in Camping

A car filled with four excited people and lots of camping gear turned by the sign that said "Campground." Hank was driving. His girlfriend, Holly, sat next to him in the front seat.

Hank and Holly began dating in high school and have been dating for four years now. They are both 21 years old.

Hank's brother, John, was in the back seat. John is 22 years old. John's girlfriend, Jessica, who is 21 years old, sat next to him in the back seat.

John and Hank grew up camping with their family. They liked to be outside. The brothers were both happy to show their girlfriends all they knew about camping.

Jessica and John have Down syndrome. They met eight months ago at a walk to raise money for a local Down syndrome program. John was walking in front of Jessica and she noticed him right away. He had a great laugh and was very stylishly dressed. Jessica knew a lot about style and fashion.

When John stopped to tie his shoe, she walked up to him and pretended she needed to tie her shoe, too. She said, "Hi, I'm Jessica."

John looked up and smiled. He thought Jessica was pretty. She had a beautiful smile and shiny, brown hair. John liked shiny, brown hair.

John said, "I'm John. Those are my friends up there. Do you want to walk with us?" Jessica walked with John and his friends for the rest of the walk, but they only talked to each other.

They exchanged phone numbers. Two days later, Jessica called John. She asked him if he wanted to go feed the ducks at a park.

John met Jessica at the park. They fed the ducks. They smiled and laughed and decided they would be boyfriend and girlfriend.

Eight months later, Jessica and John were on their way to their first overnight date. They held hands in the back seat of the car. In the front seat, Holly and Hank talked about their favorite music.

Hank said he liked country music. Holly laughed because she thinks country music is silly and "twangy." She likes dance music. John heard Holly laughing about country music.

"Country music is the best!" said John.

"Amen, brother," said Hank.

"Okay, so you guys like country music. What about you, Jessica? What kind of music do you like?" Holly asked Jessica.

"Well," Jessica said, "I like lots of music. My favorite singer is Frank Sinatra. That's what my mom and dad listen to, and I know all his songs. I also like The Beach Boys because...."

"Watch out for the raccoon!" Holly shouted.

Hank made a very sharp right turn so he would not hit the large raccoon in the middle of the road. Everyone held their breath. The car did not hit the raccoon. But the car did run over a patch of gravel, spin around, knock over a small tree, and land in a ditch.

"Is everyone okay?" Hank asked.

"Yes, we're okay," Jessica said. "I'm glad we were wearing our seatbelts."

Holly looked at Hank. She knew he was going to be upset about his car. Hank tried to drive the car out of the ditch. The wheels turned, but the car didn't go anywhere. "Would you like us to get out and push?" Holly asked Hank.

"Sure," he said.

Holly, John, and Jessica got out and put their hands on the back of the car. Holly yelled, "Okay, go!"

Hank pressed the gas pedal. Holly, Jessica, and John pushed as hard as they could but the car didn't move an inch. They tried five more times, but the car did not move at all.

Hank got out of the car and looked at the dent in his car's back bumper. Hank frowned. He put his hands in his pockets and shook his head.

"Sorry, Hank," said John.

"Me too, John. Me too," Hank replied. "It's going to get dark in a couple hours. We can walk to the campground in about ten minutes.

"Let's grab as much stuff as we can and walk the rest of the way. I will call a tow truck to pull the car out of the ditch in the morning."

Everyone nodded. They loaded their arms with camping gear: tents, sleeping bags, a lantern, and backpacks filled with clothes, food, water bottles, and flashlights. Then they started walking toward the campsite.

Jessica and John walked ahead of Holly and Hank. John asked, "Have you ever been in a car crash, Jessica?"

"No. That was scary!" Jessica said. "Have you been in a car crash before?"

"When I was a little boy we got in a car crash at the mall parking lot. My dad said it was just a 'fender bender' but my mom was mad!" John said. Then John and Jessica heard Hank and Holly fighting.

"*Just a car?!*" Hank yelled.

"Yes, *just a car*. We're all okay and that's the most important thing," said Holly.

Hank said, "That's easy for you to say. You didn't work and save up money to buy your car like I did. Your parents bought your car for you."

"So what?" Holly asked.

"Well, I'm just saying that your parents have given you everything, including your fancy red car! You have never had a job. You are a little spoiled, if you ask me. I have worked and saved my money for the things I have," Hank said.

"Did you just call me *spoiled*? That is so unfair! You shouldn't be mean to me just because you are upset about your car!" Holly said.

"I am not being mean. I'm just telling the truth. If *your* car had to be fixed, your parents would just pay for it. Well, guess what? My mom and dad cannot give me money to fix my car," Hank said.

"Now I will have to work more hours at the bookstore. I will have a dent in my stupid fender until I save enough money to fix it!" Hank yelled.

"I never said you shouldn't be upset about your car. I said the most important thing is that we are all okay! No one was hurt. I think people are more important than a stupid car!" Holly yelled back.

"Oh, now my car is stupid?" Hank asked.

Jessica and John looked at each other. "Let's walk faster," Jessica said. "I don't want to listen to fighting." John nodded his head.

As they walked, Jessica asked John, "Do they fight like this a lot? What if they break up?"

"Don't worry," John said. "They fight like this sometimes. But they always make up. My dad says it is okay for couples to disagree."

"John, I don't want to fight with you," Jessica said as they arrived at the campsite.

"Me neither," said John as he put down the things he was carrying.

Jessica and John began setting up their tent. John had done this many times, so the tent went up quickly. Jessica and John crawled inside with their things. They arranged their sleeping bags next to each other. Then they began unpacking their backpacks.

Jessica saw John's pajamas and started laughing. "John, your pajamas don't match!" Jessica said. "The pants have basketballs on them, but your top is striped. The colors don't even match!" Jessica kept giggling. She thought this was very funny.

John shrugged. He said, "I'm just sleeping in them. I don't care if they match." Then he smiled and said, "Okay Jessica, let me see your pajamas."

Jessica reached into her backpack and pulled out her pajamas. They were purple and shiny and very pretty. "See," Jessica said. "They match!"

John said, "Uh huh." He was thinking about how pretty Jessica would look in her purple pajamas when he heard Hank throw his camping gear down near their tent.

Jessica and John crawled out of their tent. Holly was taking the food out of bags and putting it on the picnic table. She and Hank were not speaking to each other.

"Um," John said, "Jessica and I are going to get firewood."

"Do you mind if I go with you?" asked Holly. Jessica and John nodded.

As they walked away to find firewood, Holly said, "I'm really sorry, you guys. I'm sorry that Hank and I are fighting on your first camping trip together.

"It will be okay," Holly continued. "I'm just so angry that he thinks I am spoiled. He thinks he is the only one who has ever had to work hard for anything! I know he works hard at the bookstore. Believe me, he tells me all the time!"

Jessica said, "I work very hard in school."

"*Great point!*" Holly said very loudly. Then she turned around and walked quickly toward the campsite.

Jessica and John stopped. Soon they heard Holly shouting toward Hank.

"Hank! Jessica just made an excellent point," Holly said.

Jessica looked at John and wondered what Holly was about to say. They followed Holly back to the campsite.

Holly said, "Hank, school has always been very easy for you. You barely have to study for tests. I work very hard and study so much more than you do. But you still get better grades than I do!"

Holly was very upset. She said, "Plus, Jessica and John work really hard in school too. So you're not the only one who knows how it feels to work hard!"

Hank was putting up his tent and did not say a word. Jessica was uncomfortable. She tugged on John's arm and said, "Let's go get firewood."

John was about to head into the woods with Jessica when he saw something moving on top of the picnic table. It was another raccoon!

"Hank," John got his brother's attention. "Do you see that?" John pointed toward the raccoon. It was headed for the chocolate bars they would use to make S'mores. Jessica was shocked that John was so calm.

"What are you going to do?" Jessica asked in a whisper. But John did not answer her. He and Hank had been camping many times. They had seen many raccoons trying to steal their dinner.

Both brothers ran to their backpacks and returned with flashlights. Then they looked at each other and nodded their heads. At the same time, they turned on their flashlights and pointed them at the raccoon.

But this raccoon was not scared by the flashlight beams. He was now trying to open the plastic bag with the chocolate bars.

Hank huffed and said, "I'm not going to let another raccoon ruin our camping trip. I hope you guys like raccoon stew, because I'm going to get this little thief!"

Hank picked up a rock and began walking toward the raccoon. Just as he was ready to throw the rock, Hank tripped on a branch and landed on the ground. He made a loud "oomph!" sound.

The noise of Hank tripping was enough to scare away the raccoon. It was also enough to make John, Jessica, and Holly laugh.

They laughed hard. John pretended he was falling too. Holly laughed so hard that she cried. Finally, Hank began to laugh too.

"All right you guys," he said. "Very funny, very funny! Let's see how you would feel if you tripped and fell in the dirt."

"Do you think you are the only one who has ever tripped before?" Holly said. She was still laughing, but Hank knew she was talking about their fight.

"Fine," Hank said. "You have all tripped and fallen before, *and* you have all worked hard. I know I'm not the only one who works hard."

Hank began to brush the leaves and dirt off his clothes. Holly walked over to him and brushed the dirt off his shoulders. It was clear that she was no longer angry with him.

Holly said, "I really am sorry about your car." Hank kissed her quickly on the cheek. Jessica and John were glad to see that Hank and Holly were no longer fighting.

Hank said, "Man, I'm hungry. Let's go see if the raccoon got away with any of our food. Maybe we can start dinner."

Hank and Holly walked over to the picnic table.

While sorting through the food, Hank said, "John, how about you and Jessica go get that firewood now? We need to start a fire to roast the hot dogs."

As he turned around, Hank saw that John and Jessica already had the same idea.

They were walking down the path together, holding hands. John said something about purple pajamas. Then they turned a corner in the path and disappeared from sight.

That night, Jessica, John, Holly, and Hank roasted hot dogs and made S'mores. They took turns telling jokes and stories. Everyone laughed a lot. No one saw any more raccoons.

What Do You Think?

1. In this story, Hank saved the money he made from his job so he could buy a car. Is it easy or hard for you to save money? Are you saving money for anything special?

2. Have you ever been around people who were fighting or yelling at each other? What did it feel like?

3. Do you like to go camping? What is your favorite part of camping?

4. Jessica and John slept in a tent together. Hank and Holly slept in a separate tent together. What do you think about boyfriends and girlfriends sleeping in the same tent together?

Dear Diary

Dear Diary,

Today it is 56 degrees and very windy.

I am going to see Ramon tonight. He's been my boyfriend for over five months now.

We have a lot of fun together. We like a lot of the same things. We both like softball, singing, scary movies, and blue raspberry slushies from the gas station.

But there are some things that we don't have in common. Ramon really likes to dance, but I do not. I feel like everyone is looking at me when I dance. It makes me nervous.

Sometimes Ramon talks too much. Sometimes I just want him to be quiet, but he keeps talking and talking and talking. I try to ignore it, though. I'm glad to have a boyfriend who goes to the movies with me and holds my hand.

We are going to see a movie tonight. Ramon said it's really scary!

∽

Dear Diary,

Today it is 48 degrees. I had to wear a scarf on my way to the bus stop.

Ramon and I are still dating. It is going okay, but sometimes I think he talks to other women too much. I know he just likes to talk, but I wish he wouldn't talk to Angela.

Angela wants Ramon to be her boyfriend. But he is *my* boyfriend, not hers. I told Ramon that I don't like Angela, but he doesn't care. He talks to her anyway. I don't think that's very nice. It makes me sad.

Tomorrow night we are going to a party at the Park of Roses. I think I will wear a rose in my hair. I hope I can find a yellow one. My dad always tells me I look pretty in yellow.

Dear Diary,

Today it is 63 degrees. It is nice and sunny outside.

I don't feel so nice and sunny. Last night Ramon and I got into a fight at the Park of Roses party.

When one of our favorite songs came on I asked Ramon to sit next to me and sing along. Ramon said he would rather dance. That made me sad.

I had even worn my pretty blue dress and had a yellow tulip in my hair. (I couldn't find a yellow rose, but the man at the grocery store said that yellow tulips are also very pretty.) All I wanted was for Ramon to sit and hold my hand.

Ramon knows that I don't like to dance. But he went to the dance floor anyway. Guess who he danced with? Angela!

I was so upset that I wouldn't talk to him when he came back to the table. He kept asking me what was wrong. I told him that he knows I don't like it when he talks to Angela.

He said he wasn't talking — he was dancing. I told him it didn't matter! Angela was dancing too close, and he should have stopped her.

I told him that isn't how a boyfriend should behave. He said he didn't do anything wrong. I didn't know what else to say, so I blurted out, "I want to break up with you!"

Now we are broken up. I called him this morning but he didn't answer. I miss him.

〰️

Dear Diary,

Today it is 62 degrees and rainy.

It has been raining for the last three days. I have been crying for the last three days.

Ramon won't talk to me. I want to tell him I am sorry. I know I am the one who said I wanted to break up, but I don't want to be broken up.

I passed him in the hallway at work today. He was talking to his friend Danny. He just ignored me. That really hurt my feelings.

❀

Dear Diary,

Today it is 67 degrees and rainy and sunny and then rainy again.

I decided that if Ramon was going to be rude to me, then I would stop trying to talk to him. It is hard to do. I really want to talk to him. I want to tell him how sad I am.

I'm also starting to feel angry. Why doesn't Ramon care that I'm upset?

My friend Peter says that Ramon should be nicer to me, even if we are broken up. Peter says that Ramon isn't being a gentleman. I think Peter is right.

At the end of the day, Ramon waved to me before he got on the bus. I waved back.

I wasn't sure how I felt after that. Maybe Ramon will talk to me at work tomorrow.

∞

Dear Diary,

Today it is 70 degrees and cloudy.

Today, at lunch, I talked to my friends Peter and Nori. I told them that Ramon waved to me yesterday. But I was still mad at him for ignoring me all those days before.

Nori said she was mad at him, too. Peter said he would never ignore anyone. He said it is rude. I agree with Peter.

Then I saw Ramon in the hallway after lunch. He was talking to Danny again. He did not talk to me, but I did not want to talk to him either. I just kept walking. I plan to tell Nori and Peter about it tomorrow.

∞

Dear Diary,

Today it is 62 degrees and windy and cloudy.

Last night I talked with my brother, Kevin. I told him about me and Ramon breaking up and how Ramon has been rude to me.

Kevin said I acted impulsively when I broke up with Ramon. Kevin said that means I should have taken more time to think before I told Ramon that I wanted to break up.

But Kevin also said that Ramon did not act maturely. He said that Ramon was not being a gentleman. Just like Peter said.

At lunch today I told Nori and Peter that I didn't like Ramon anymore. I said I would not be mean to him, but I didn't care that we were broken up anymore.

Nori and Peter clapped their hands for me. That made me feel good.

⌇

Dear Diary,

Today it is still 62 degrees and windy but the sun is trying to come out.

Last night I thought about how it felt to be someone's girlfriend. Mostly, I liked it. Ramon and I had a lot of fun together. But, I didn't like it when Ramon paid attention to Angela. It made me angry and it made me wonder if Angela was better than I am.

I don't think it should be like that when you have a boyfriend.

Someday, I want to have a new boyfriend. But, for now, I would rather hang out with my friends.

Tomorrow is supposed to be 72 degrees and sunny. It will be a beautiful day. I will ask Nori and Peter if they want to eat lunch outside with me.

There are yellow tulips in the garden at work. Maybe I'll ask if I can pick some to take home.

What Do You Think?

1. What is a diary? Why would someone write in a diary?

2. In the story, Ramon danced with Angela even though his girlfriend did not want him to. Do you think it was okay for Ramon to dance with Angela? Do you think it was okay for the girlfriend to not like Angela?

3. Ramon's girlfriend got very mad at him. What do you do when you get mad?

4. Have you ever broken up with a boyfriend or girlfriend? What was it like?

5. Have you ever been ignored? How did that make you feel?

A Very Lucky Dog

1. Tucker

Kasey could not sleep. She kept thinking about what she was going to name her new dog.

In the morning, Kasey was going to the dog shelter to pick up the dog she chose two days ago. There were many dogs in the shelter that were waiting to be adopted. Kasey chose her dog because he seemed to be smiling at her as she walked past him.

She had never seen a dog smile before.

"Maybe I will name him Smokey. Or maybe Pepper. Or Dutch," Kasey thought as she lay in bed. She was very excited to have a dog. She had always wanted a dog. Now she thought the time was right.

Last month, she began her new job as a nurse. Now she would have money to pay for all the things a dog needs. She moved into a house with a small backyard with a fence around it. Now she would have a place for her dog to play. Kasey had thought of everything.

Kasey's grandpa did not think getting a dog was a good idea. Kasey talked to her grandpa about any big decisions she made. She loved her grandpa and thought he was very smart.

Two days ago, she called her grandpa to tell him about the dog she found at the dog shelter. Kasey lay in bed and remembered the phone call.

"Kasey, do you really want the responsibility of a dog?" her grandpa asked.

"Yes, Grandpa. You know I have always wanted a dog," Kasey said.

"I know. But remember this dog is going to take up a lot of your time. You are already on your feet all day as a nurse, and you will have to walk the dog every night when you get home from work. Plus, I worry about you walking alone at night."

Kasey's grandpa continued, "Dogs also cost a lot of money. He will need food, toys, and tags with his name and address. Don't forget about a collar and leash. Do you know how much vet bills cost?"

"Grandpa," Kasey said, "I've saved money for those things. I've thought of everything. I am ready. I really want a dog."

"I know you do. Dogs can make a person very happy. Did I ever tell you about my dog, Tucker? I had him before I married your grandmother. He was a funny dog with one blue eye and one brown eye. But he was a lot of work!" he said.

"I remember you talking about Tucker. Now I want my own dog," she said.

"Okay, Kasey. I just want you to be happy," he said.

Now, it was two days later and she would have her new dog in the morning. As Kasey lay in bed, she had a great idea. She decided she would name her new dog Tucker, just like her grandpa's old dog.

"Grandpa will love that," Kasey thought. Then she fell asleep.

The next morning, Kasey rushed over to the dog shelter to pick up Tucker. She was thrilled to see him again and Tucker was just as excited! Kasey felt happy and sure about her choice to adopt Tucker.

Tucker was half Pug and half Shar-Pei. He was a small dog with brown and black fur, a short, curly tail, and a very flat nose. Also, he had three legs instead of four.

The people at the dog shelter told Kasey that Tucker had been hit by a car.

Many of the bones in his back left leg were broken. He would not be able to walk on this leg again. So the dog shelter removed the leg.

Once he healed, they helped Tucker learn to walk on three legs. They told Kasey that the dog was very lucky to have lived through the accident.

The people at the dog shelter also told Kasey that Tucker was extremely energetic and, like all dogs, he would need a lot of exercise. Kasey thought to herself that surely a dog with three legs would need less exercise than a dog with four legs.

Kasey did not like to exercise often. Plus her new home had a backyard with room for Tucker to run around by himself. Perhaps she would not need to walk him *every* night. Kasey thought she had it all figured out.

After she filled out all the paperwork to adopt Tucker, Kasey and her new dog went to the pet supply store to make a name tag for him. Kasey put her phone number on the tag. In case Tucker got lost, the person who found him could call Kasey on the phone. Kasey had thought of everything for her new dog.

The first night Tucker spent with Kasey was not what she expected. Instead of curling up in the corner of his crate, Tucker yelped and whined all night.

After three more nights like this, Kasey was very tired and frustrated. So she decided she would let Tucker sleep with her.

All the books that Kasey had read about dogs said that owners should not let their dogs sleep in bed with them. But she was too tired to care what the books said anymore. She needed a good night's sleep.

That is exactly what she got the first night Tucker slept in Kasey's bed. Neither Kasey nor Tucker moved once during the night.

"I slept really well last night. How about you, Tucker?" Kasey smiled at Tucker as she talked to him, and Tucker wagged his tail. They were becoming good friends.

Tucker was a very smart dog, Kasey could tell. He was house trained very quickly. He learned to obey commands like "sit," "lay down," and "roll over" within a week.

Tucker's favorite game was chasing his rope toy when Kasey threw it. Kasey's arm always got tired from throwing the toy before Tucker was ready to stop playing. Kasey was surprised by how much energy Tucker had!

"Geez, I didn't think a dog with three legs would be so active," Kasey said to herself one day. Then she had a clever idea.

Kasey hired someone to put a doggie door in her back door. Now, Tucker could get outside and run around in the fenced-in backyard whenever he wanted.

Kasey was pleased with her good idea. She was pleased that Tucker could play and be happy while she was at work. She was also pleased that she wouldn't need to spend so much time exercising with Tucker when she came home in the evenings.

"You can run around all day and be ready for bed by the time I get home. Right, Tucker?" Kasey asked him just as he was jumping through his new doggie door. Now, Kasey had truly thought of everything.

Or, so she thought.

2. Lost

Two weeks after the doggie door was put in, Kasey came home from work and could not find Tucker.

She called his name inside and outside.

"Tucker! Tucker! Come here boy! Tucker! I have a treat for you!"

Still, no Tucker. Kasey was worried. Where was her dog? She walked in and out of the back door, trying to figure out where Tucker could be.

"Tucker!" she yelled again. Kasey was standing on her back steps and looking at the fence. Then she saw it.

A tunnel just big enough for Tucker to squeeze through had been dug under the fence, right next to Tucker's favorite shady tree.

"Oh, no!" Kasey cried. She ran inside and called her grandpa.

"Grandpa, Tucker dug a hole under the fence in the backyard and he's gone! Will you help me look for him?" Kasey asked.

"Yes, of course. I will be there soon." Ten minutes later, Kasey's grandpa knocked on her front door. He gave her a big hug and handed her a flashlight.

"Good idea," Kasey said. "It is getting dark." She felt much better now that her grandpa was there.

Kasey and her grandpa spent over an hour walking around her neighborhood, calling for Tucker.

"Tucker! Here boy!" they said.

They passed two women who were taking a walk. Kasey asked them if they had seen a small dog with three legs. "His name is Tucker and he's very friendly," Kasey said. Her voice was hoarse from shouting for Tucker.

"Oh, dear, I'm sorry," said one of the women. "We have not seen any dogs like that tonight."

"Thank you anyway," Kasey's grandpa said. He put his arm around Kasey. "Tucker is my granddaughter's dog. Her phone number is on his tag if you happen to find him," he said.

"We will certainly call if we find him. Best of luck to you," one woman said as they walked away.

Kasey and her grandpa did not find Tucker that night. In the morning, Kasey called the dog shelter. She hoped someone had picked him up and taken him to the shelter during the night.

After Tucker was hit by the car a few months earlier, someone had dropped him off at the shelter in the middle of the night. But he was not at the shelter this morning.

Next, Kasey made a flyer on her computer with the words "MISSING DOG" at the top. She printed 100 copies. As the flyers were printing, Kasey's grandpa called.

"Any news?" he asked.

"No news. I made a flyer and I'm going to put copies on telephone poles. Would you post some flyers in your neighborhood, Grandpa?" she asked.

"Sure," he answered kindly.

"Thank you for your help, Grandpa. I know you didn't think I should get a dog. Maybe you were right," Kasey said.

"Kasey, there is no one else I would rather help than you. I also think you are doing a good job with Tucker, but you are still learning. We can talk more about this later. Let's go find Tucker," he said.

3. Saved

While Kasey and her grandpa were posting the "MISSING DOG" flyers all over the city, Tucker was enjoying his adventure. There were so many smells to smell and animals to chase outside Kasey's backyard. During the many hours since he crawled through the hole under the fence, Tucker had chased four cats, two mice, seven ducks, and at least twenty squirrels.

Then Tucker spotted the biggest animals he had seen yet. Next to a pond were two fat gray geese.

As he walked closer, he saw there were many geese. Some were walking around the pond and others were swimming in the pond. Tucker could not resist.

He began running toward the geese and barking as loudly as he could. Before he knew it, he was in the water, still chasing the geese. But there was a problem.

Tucker had not learned to swim with only three legs. This was harder than swimming with four legs, like most dogs do. Tucker felt himself bobbing up and down, his head going under water and then coming back up again. This was making him very tired.

He forgot the geese and swam toward the edge of the pond. His paws kicked, but he was not getting very far. His head sank under the water for a few seconds. Suddenly, he felt something grab him and pull him along.

Soon he was lying on the grassy shore next to a man who was breathing very heavily. Tucker raised his head and looked at the man. The man raised his head and looked at the dog. Then both of them laid their heads back on the grass, exhausted.

4. Lucky Dog

Kasey was stapling a "MISSING DOG" poster to a telephone pole when she heard her cell phone ring. She pulled it out of her pocket and answered, "Hello?"

"Yes, hello. My name is Bob. I believe I may have found something that belongs to you," said the man on the phone.

"My dog? Do you have my dog, Tucker?!" Kasey asked. Her heart began racing.

"Yes, I believe I have Tucker here," he answered.

"Oh, thank you, thank you," Kasey said. "Where are you?"

"I am at Weeping Willow Park. Do you know where that is?" he asked.

"I think so. I will meet you there as soon as I can," she said. "Thank you again."

Then Kasey called her grandpa to tell him the good news.

"Oh Kasey, that is wonderful! Do you know where Weeping Willow Park is?" he asked.

"I think so, but I haven't been there in a long time," she answered.

"I know where it is. Why don't I drive you? Your house is on the way," he said.

"Okay, Grandpa, see you soon!" Kasey said.

After several minutes in the car together, Kasey and her grandpa were three miles away from Weeping Willow Park. Kasey said, "I can't believe Tucker ran this far away! He must have traveled almost ten miles."

"Yes, that dog has a lot of energy. You know, Kasey, Tucker will need more exercise than he was getting before," Kasey's grandpa said gently.

Kasey wanted to remind her grandpa that she threw the rope toy to Tucker almost every night. She wanted to remind him that she put in a doggie door so he could go outside while she was at work. But the more she learned about Tucker, the more she realized that he did need a lot of exercise—a lot more exercise than she had thought.

Kasey had *not* thought of everything, after all.

"I know, Grandpa," Kasey said quietly. A couple minutes later they pulled into the parking lot at Weeping Willow Park.

Kasey saw a man sitting on a bench with Tucker lying by his feet. Kasey burst out of the car and yelled "Tucker? Is that you?"

Tucker stood up, shook off some water, and walked over to Kasey with his tail wagging. Kasey bent down and gave Tucker a big hug. "I'm so happy to see you! I was so worried about you!" Kasey said. She stood up and looked at the man standing next to her grandpa.

The man said, "I'm Bob. It is nice to meet you." Then he shook hands with Kasey and her grandpa.

"We're so grateful that you found Tucker. My name is Gene and this is my granddaughter Kasey. We've been looking for Tucker since yesterday evening," Kasey's grandpa said. "I see that you are both wet. Did you go for a swim?"

Bob laughed a little. Then he said, "No, not quite. I was sitting on a bench reading the newspaper when I heard your dog barking at the geese. By the time I stood up, he had jumped into the water."

Then Bob looked at Tucker and said, "You will never catch a goose in the water, silly dog. They are much faster swimmers than dogs." Bob bent down to pet Tucker.

"After a few seconds I noticed that your dog seemed to be having some trouble swimming. I could tell he was kicking, but his head kept going under water. I was afraid he was going to drown. So I jumped in the water and grabbed him," Bob said.

"Thank you so much! Thank you for swimming in that yucky pond to save my dog," Kasey said to Bob. Then she looked at Tucker, who was starting to sniff around on the ground. "Tucker, you are a very lucky dog!"

"Do you know if Tucker can swim?" Bob asked Kasey.

"I don't know. I assume he could swim before he lost his hind leg. But I have not taken him swimming since I got him at the shelter. Aren't dogs with three legs able to swim?" Kasey asked.

Bob shrugged his shoulders and said, "I bet Tucker can learn to swim. But you may want to get him some swimming lessons before he starts chasing geese again!"

Everyone laughed. "Swimming lessons are a good idea," said Kasey. "I have to figure out a way to get Tucker more exercise, that's for sure. I will start by taking him on a long walk every night."

Bob said, "I think there are a few doggie daycares in town. My neighbor takes her dog to one.

She said her dog runs around all day with other dogs and is worn out for days afterward."

"Would you like to go to doggie daycare?" Kasey asked Tucker. He wagged his tail. "I think he said 'Yes,'" Kasey said with a smile.

Kasey's grandpa said, "I have a feeling that will not be cheap, Kasey."

"Probably not," she said. "But I have been saving for a new TV. I think it would be better to use that money for Tucker."

"Good idea," he said.

Kasey looked at Bob and his wet clothes. "Bob, I hope your clothes are not ruined. Can I pay for your dry cleaning bill?"

Bob shook his head and said, "Thank you for offering, but I'm not worried about these old clothes. I am happy I was able to help." Bob paused and then he smiled. "I had a dog once. She was a collie, like Lassie."

"Oh, collies are beautiful dogs," Kasey's grandpa said. "You know I had a dog once, too. His name was Tucker, just like our little swimmer here...."

Bob and Kasey and Kasey's grandpa sat in the park and exchanged dog stories for a few more minutes. Tucker barked at a few geese. Kasey thanked Bob for saving Tucker a few more times.

Tucker was a very lucky dog indeed.

What Do You Think?

1. Have you ever owned a pet? What kind of pet?

2. What is fun about having a pet? What is hard about having a pet?

3. Kasey did not think that Tucker would have as much energy as he did. She underestimated his energy level. Why? Has anyone ever underestimated you?

4. In this story, Kasey's grandpa helped her a lot. Do you think she should have looked for Tucker on her own? Do you think she was right to ask her grandpa for help?

5. Have you ever been lost? What did it feel like?

Dirty Dishes

"What's that smell?" Claire thought to herself as she walked into her apartment. She had just spent the weekend with her parents.

Claire hung up her coat and took off her boots. She wondered why her apartment smelled like cheese, bananas, and rotten eggs all at the same time.

As she walked into the kitchen, she saw more dirty dishes than she had ever seen before.

The kitchen sink was full of dirty dishes. The countertop was covered in dirty dishes. There were even dirty pots and pans stacked on top of the stove.

Right away, Claire thought about her roommate, Elaine. Elaine must have used every single plate, bowl, cup, pot, and pan in the entire kitchen!

Claire liked to keep things nice and neat. Her bedroom was always tidy. She always washed her dishes after she used them.

But Elaine was not like Claire. Elaine didn't mind dirty dishes or dusty bookshelves. Her bedroom was so messy that you couldn't see the floor. It was covered by dirty laundry, piles of papers, bags, boxes, and more dirty dishes!

Claire didn't even like to look at Elaine's bedroom. But Claire never said anything to Elaine about her messiness.

She and Elaine had become close friends since they moved into their apartment together.

Claire was afraid she would upset Elaine if she told her how she really felt. So instead, Claire always cleaned the messes that Elaine made.

Claire stood in the kitchen and looked at all the dirty dishes. She thought about what she could say to Elaine when she came home: "Why didn't you wash any of these dishes?" "I wish you would have cleaned the kitchen before you left for work." "These dirty dishes make our apartment smell like old cheese!"

But what if Elaine got mad at Claire for confronting her? Claire worried that Elaine wouldn't want to be her friend anymore. So, as usual, Claire rolled up her sleeves and started cleaning Elaine's mess.

She decided to start with the sink first. Claire liked to wash dishes in a certain order: silverware, cups and glasses, plates and bowls, then pots and pans. This was the order that her mother taught her.

Claire thought her mother was the kindest, smartest, and cleanest person she had ever known. Her parents didn't live very far away, and whenever they came for a visit, Claire wanted her apartment to be "spick-and-span," as her mom liked to say.

She began washing the knives, forks, and spoons. As she dug her hand below a stack of plates to grab a spoon, a bug crawled across her hand.

She howled and yanked her hand out of the sink. Then she ran out of the kitchen into the hallway. Claire was breathing quickly. "Yuck, yuck, yuck!" she shouted.

From around the corner, Claire watched the bug. It crawled across the counter and down the cabinet. It was headed for the hallway. She was sure this was the biggest, fastest, and grossest bug she had ever seen.

Then Claire thought, "What if it crawls into one of my boots in the hallway?" She didn't want to go near the nasty bug, but she didn't want it to crawl into any of her shoes either.

"I'm going to trap you. Don't move," Claire said to the bug.

Claire went into the kitchen and grabbed the biggest pot she could find. When she came back, she found the bug in the middle of the hallway. She turned the pot upside down and put it on top of the bug. Now the bug was trapped under the heavy pot.

"Phew!" said Claire. She was proud of herself for trapping the bug, and she thought her mother would be proud, too. Claire's heart was beating quickly. She went into the living room to sit in her favorite chair and calm down.

As she sat, she got angry. She was tired of cleaning Elaine's messes. Claire thought to herself, "Elaine never cleans up after herself because she knows I will do it! She's so lazy! Now there are gross bugs!"

A moment later, the front door opened. Elaine walked in with her staff person, Donna. They both sniffed the air and made squishy faces like they smelled something really bad.

Donna asked, "What have you ladies been cooking in here? Rotten egg stew?"

Claire was too angry to say hello to Donna or Elaine. She was too angry to say anything. Then Elaine asked, "Why is that pot upside down on the floor?"

Claire had an idea.

"Elaine, you should pick it up and find out," Claire said as calmly as she could.

Elaine bent down, picked up the pot, and the bug ran across her shoe!

Elaine screamed and threw the pot into the air. The pot landed on the floor with a loud clanging sound. Donna screamed too. She jumped onto a chair to stay out of the bug's way. Claire stood in the living room and watched.

"Why did you do that, Claire?!" shouted Elaine. "That bug just crawled across my shoe! That wasn't funny at all!"

"Quick!" Donna said. "We have to catch the bug before it crawls into another room!"

Donna grabbed a magazine from the kitchen table, Elaine grabbed the pot, and Claire grabbed a broom. The three women tip-toed toward the bug. It was in the middle of the hall and it looked like it was staring at them.

As they walked slowly toward the bug, it started to run away from them. Claire yelled, "Elaine, try to put the pot on top of it!"

"I can't! I'm too scared," Elaine said.

"Try anyway!" Claire demanded.

Elaine held her breath and walked toward the bug. The bug was now at the front door. Donna said, "Elaine, open the door. Maybe it will run outside."

Elaine opened the front door, but the bug started running back toward the kitchen.

Claire was fed up. Poking at the bug with her broom, she forced the bug back toward the front door. Then, with a firm whack of the broom, Claire shoved the big bug outside. She shut the door.

Everyone breathed a sigh of relief.

"That was so gross! I need a rest," said Elaine.

"Not so fast," Claire said. "Look at the kitchen. Look at all your dirty dishes. That bug was in the sink under those dirty dishes! This is your fault!"

Claire couldn't believe she had just said that to her friend. Suddenly, she became very nervous that Elaine would be mad at her. She wanted to apologize, but Donna started talking.

"Claire is right, Elaine. You made this mess, and it is your job to clean it up. Plus, remember what we talked about when you first moved into your apartment. Bugs love dirty apartments!" Donna said as she carried the big, bug-trapping pot back into the kitchen.

"I will help if you want," said Claire, although she didn't feel like helping.

Elaine was quiet for a few seconds. Then she asked, "If I wash the dishes, will you dry them?"

Claire nodded. The two roommates said goodbye to Donna and then got to work.

As Claire dried the dishes, she looked over each piece carefully. She didn't think Elaine was getting the dishes clean enough. So she told Elaine that she should use hotter water.

"I know how to wash dishes," Elaine snapped.

"But you *never* wash the dishes," replied Claire. "I wash them and I get them clean like my mom showed me. She said hot water is best."

Claire was finally standing up for herself and it felt good. She added, "It's also easier to get dishes clean if you wash them right after you're done eating."

"*You* should wash the dishes if you're so good at it," Elaine said.

"These are your dishes! It's not fair if I have to wash them!" Claire cried.

Then the two women were silent. Claire was nervous. But she believed that Elaine was wrong. So she decided not to apologize. Neither one said anything for almost five minutes.

"Okay, fine," Elaine said at last. But I'm not going to wash your dishes too."

"So *you* will wash *your* dishes and *I* will wash *mine*?" asked Claire.

"Yes," said Elaine.

Suddenly, Elaine started to laugh. "Did you see Donna jump up on the chair?"

Claire giggled. "Yes! That was so funny! I thought she was going to jump on the kitchen table!"

Then Elaine got quiet. "Claire, I'm sorry about the dishes. I hope we don't see any more bugs like that. It was gross." Elaine squished up her face as she thought about the big bug. "Do you forgive me?" asked Elaine.

"Yes, I forgive you," said Claire. She gave Elaine a quick hug. Claire and Elaine continued to wash and dry dishes for another thirty minutes.

Elaine was the first to yawn. That made Claire yawn. Then neither of them could stop yawning.

By the time they were finished washing dishes, their hands were wrinkly from the water and their legs were tired from standing so long.

Later that night, after a hot bath, Claire lay in bed and thought about her friend Elaine and the big bug. She smiled as she remembered how she had been the one to shove the bug outside. Claire decided she would call her mom the next day and tell her all about it.

What Do You Think?

1. Have you ever lived with a messy person? How did you feel about that?

2. Is it easy or hard to keep *your* space clean?

3. What would you do if you found a bug in your room?

4. Have you ever been angry at a friend?

5. At the end of the story, Claire and Elaine talk about why they are mad at each other. Was this a good or bad way to end the fight?

The Kissing Scene

Cast of Characters:
1. Dana
2. Drew
3. Susan
4. Simon
5. Wendy
6. Will
7. Megan
8. Molly

There is also a Narrator. This person tells the readers what the characters are doing. The narrator reads all *italicized*, or *slanted*, words.

<u>Narrator</u>: *Today, six people are trying out for parts in a play. A play is a story that is acted out on stage. This play is about two people named Becky and Brian.*

The Director of the play is Megan. She will pick the two people who do the best job pretending to be Becky and Brian.

Three women (Dana, Susan, and Wendy) want to play Becky and three men (Drew, Simon, and Will) want to play Brian. They are waiting behind the stage for their turn to try out in front of Megan. Later, Megan will talk about the try-outs with her partner, Molly.

<u>Narrator</u>: *Dana and Drew are sitting across from each other. They are friends with each other through work.*

<u>Dana</u>: Drew, I am really nervous. I can't even remember what this play is about!

Drew: Dana, we are going to try out in a few minutes! How could you forget what the play is about?

Dana: I forget things when I am nervous!

Drew: Okay, here is what you need to know. The two people in this play are Becky and Brian. Becky and Brian have been friends for almost twenty years. They have gone through a lot of sad and happy times together.

In the part we are playing today, Becky and Brian are having coffee together. Becky tells Brian that she is sorry about his divorce from his wife.

Then Becky tells Brian that she would like to be his girlfriend. Brian thinks this is a good idea. Then they lean across the table in the coffee shop and kiss each other.

Dana: Thanks. I remember now. I am nervous about the kissing part. We have not practiced that part.

Drew: I am a little nervous about the kissing part too. My wife, Diane, is the only person I have ever kissed.

Dana: Is she okay with you kissing me for the play?

Drew: She said it is fine, as long as I do not enjoy it. [Drew and Dana both laugh.]

Narrator: *On the other side of the room, Susan and Simon are practicing for their turn to try out for the roles of Becky and Brian. Susan and Simon are not nervous about the kissing part of the play because they are dating each other. They have already kissed many times.*

Simon: Maybe we should practice the kiss one more time.

Susan: I think we have kissed enough. We should keep practicing the words. I want to play the part of Becky better than anyone else!

Simon: I think Becky is a good kisser. We should keep working on that part.

Susan: Ha, ha. Okay, one more kiss.

Narrator: *Susan smiles and kisses Simon.*

Narrator: *Will opens the door to the practice area and runs inside. He is late. He finds Wendy sitting quietly.*

Will: I am so sorry, Wendy! I woke up late and missed the bus.

Wendy: No p-p-p-problem.

Narrator: *Wendy closes her eyes and takes some deep breaths. Sometimes Wendy repeats the first sound of words and it is hard for her to say what she wants to say. This is called stuttering.*

<u>Wendy</u>: S-s-s-s-sorry, my stuttering gets worse when I am n-n-nervous.

<u>Will</u>: Don't worry about that, Wendy. Once we get out on stage, we are going to be great! Do you want to practice the lines one more time?

<u>Narrator</u>: *Wendy nods. Wendy and Will met at their book club two months ago. Wendy saw that Will had her favorite book, "Where the Red Fern Grows," in his book bag. She asked him if he liked the book. Will said it was one of the best books he had ever read. They have been friends ever since.*

<u>Narrator</u>: *Megan, the Director of the play, walks into the room.*

<u>Megan</u>: Okay, Drew and Dana, it is your turn.

<u>Narrator</u>: *Drew and Dana walk onto the stage. Megan sits down in the front row to watch them.*

<u>Megan</u>: Remember, we are starting at the part when Becky tells Brian that she is sorry about his divorce. Are you ready?

Dana: Yes, we are ready.

Megan: Okay, action!

Narrator: *A table and two chairs are on the stage. Dana and Drew sit down across from each other.*

Dana [playing Becky]: Brian, I am sorry you and your ex-wife could not stay together. Divorce can be hard.

When my brother got divorced, he was sad for a while. Then he started dating again. Now he has a new girlfriend. I saw a picture of them on Facebook yesterday and he looked very happy.

Drew [playing Brian]: I'm not on Facebook. Maybe I should join.

Dana [playing Becky]: For sure! Facebook is a great way to stay in touch with friends. My cousin got back in touch with her old high school boyfriend on Facebook. Now they are dating again!

Drew [playing Brian]: I have been thinking about what it would be like to go on a date again.

Dana [playing Becky]: What do you think about going on a date with me?

Drew [playing Brian]: Do you mean like right now, having coffee together?

Dana [playing Becky]: Not exactly. I think I would like to be more than friends with you, Brian. I would like to be your girlfriend.

Drew [playing Brian]: Really? I thought you only wanted to be friends with me.

Dana [playing Becky]: Not anymore.

Drew [playing Brian]: Well, that is good news! I think I would like to be your boyfriend. How should we start?

Dana [playing Becky]: How about a kiss?

Narrator: *Dana [playing Becky] leans across the table and gives Drew [playing Brian] a kiss on the lips.*

Megan: Great job! Thank you both. I will let you know tomorrow if you get to play Becky and Brian. Will you please ask Susan and Simon to come to the stage for their turn?

Drew: Sure. Thank you, Megan. We look forward to hearing from you!

Narrator: *Drew and Dana leave and tell Simon and Susan it is their turn. Simon and Susan walk onto the stage.*

Megan: Hi, guys. Are you ready?

Simon: Yes, we are ready.

Megan: Great. Action!

Narrator: *Susan and Simon sit down at the table on stage. They do a good job acting out the same scene as Drew and Dana. At the end of the scene,*

Susan [playing Becky] leans across the table and gives Simon [playing Brian] a kiss on the lips.

Megan: Very good! Thank you! I will call you tomorrow and let you know if you get to play Becky and Brian. Will you please ask Wendy and Will to come to the stage for their turn?

Susan: Yes, we will. But first, how did we do? Do you think you will pick Simon and me for the play?

Megan: You did very well. But it is too soon to tell you who will be chosen. Just wait for my call tomorrow.

Susan: Okay, thank you, Megan.

Narrator: *Susan and Simon leave the stage. They tell Wendy and Will it is their turn. Wendy and Will walk onto the stage and sit down at the table.*

Megan: Hi, Wendy and Will. Do you know where to start?

Wendy: Yes. We are s-s-starting at the part where Becky tells Brian that she is sorry about his divorce.

Megan: That's right. Okay, action!

Narrator: *Wendy and Will do a good job acting out the same scene. Wendy stutters a few times but not very much. At the end of the scene, Wendy [playing Becky] leans across the table and gives Will [playing Brian] a kiss on the lips.*

Megan: Thank you, Wendy. Thank you, Will. You did a great job. I will call you tomorrow to let you know if you will be in the play.

Will: Thanks, Megan! I hope you pick Wendy and me.

Megan: Well, I have a tough choice to make! I will call both of you tomorrow.

Will: Okay, thank you. Goodbye.

Narrator: *Will and Wendy walk off the stage. They stop in the practice area to put on their coats.*

Wendy: Thank you for all your help, Will. That was really fun! I think I only stuttered two times!

I've never done anything like that before. I'm so glad you asked me t-t-to do this with you. I feel so happy!

<u>Narrator</u>: *Wendy gives Will a big hug. Then Will and Wendy kiss.*

<u>Will</u>: I'm glad you had fun. But I never really cared that much about the play. I just wanted to spend time with you, Wendy. I like you a lot.

<u>Wendy</u>: Wow. Really?

<u>Will</u>: Really.

<u>Wendy</u>: I like you too, Will. I know my stuttering doesn't bother you, so I can relax when I'm with you. It's nice.

<u>Will</u>: I'm glad.

<u>Wendy</u>: Do you want to get a cup of coffee together, just like Becky and Brian?

<u>Will</u>: Yes, that would be great!

<u>Narrator</u>: *Wendy and Will walk out the door and go to a coffee shop.*

<u>Narrator</u>: *Later that night, Megan and her partner, Molly, sit on a couch. Megan has notes in her hands.*

<u>Megan</u>: Boy, this is going to be a tough choice. All three couples did a good job playing Becky and Brian.

<u>Molly</u>: Usually, you have a favorite right away. Do you like all three couples equally?

<u>Megan</u>: Well, no, they are all different. But I liked things about all three couples.

<u>Molly</u>: Like what?

<u>Megan</u>: It was clear that Dana and Drew knew each other like old friends, but they seemed very uncomfortable with the kiss.

Wendy and Will said they are friends who met two months ago. I think they like each other more than friends. You should have seen the way they kissed!

But I think I will choose Susan and Simon. They're very comfortable with each other off-stage and I think that will show on stage. They also seemed very well prepared for the audition.

<u>Molly</u>: Well, Megan, you have some phone calls to make!

Narrator: *The next day, Megan, the Director calls Wendy.*

Megan: Hi, Wendy, this is Megan.

Wendy: Hi, Megan.

Megan: I am calling to tell you that I picked one of the other couples to play Becky and Brian.

<u>Wendy</u>: Oh, okay.

<u>Megan</u>: But I am glad you and Will tried out for the play! You had what we call "chemistry" on stage.

<u>Wendy</u>: What does that mean?

<u>Megan</u>: It means you get along well. It seems easy for you and Will to talk to each other.

<u>Wendy</u>: I told Will the same thing yesterday!

Megan: Also, you and Will did a very nice job with the kissing part. There is a little spark between you! Well, thanks again for trying out for the play. I'm going to call Will now.

Wendy: You don't need to call him. I can tell him. He's right here next to me.

Megan: Okay, thanks. Goodbye.

Wendy: Goodbye.

Narrator: *Wendy hangs up the phone.*

Will: I'm going to guess that Megan did not choose us.

Wendy: No, she didn't.

Will: Oh, well. I think it turned out alright anyway.

Narrator: *Will gives Wendy a kiss on the cheek. Wendy smiles.*

What Do You Think?

1. Have you ever tried out for a play or a sports team before? What was it like?

2. The people trying out for the roles of Becky and Brian had to kiss, even if they were not boyfriend and girlfriend in real life. How would you feel if you had to kiss someone who was not your boyfriend or girlfriend?

3. In the play, Brian was divorced. What does that mean? Do you know anyone who got a divorce?

4. Becky tells Brian that he should go on Facebook. Are you on Facebook? What do you think of it?

5. Wendy said she could relax around Will. Why, do you think?

A Day of Kindness

Lou really wanted a dog. Every Saturday he visited the local animal shelter near his apartment. An animal shelter is where dogs and cats live while they are waiting to be adopted.

Whenever he went to the animal shelter, Lou walked around and looked at all the dogs. He would even play with a few. Lou was looking for just the right dog to take home with him.

Today, as Lou walked into the parking lot of the shelter, he saw a big tent and a sign that said, "Mingle with the Mutts." He saw many dogs meeting new people who might adopt them and take them home. The dogs wagged their tails when the people petted them. They looked very happy.

Lou really wanted a dog. He decided to go over to the tent to pet and play with the dogs.

"Where did these dogs come from?" Lou asked a woman who looked like she was in charge. "Are they all mutts?"

"Yes, they are all mutts," the kind woman answered. "For example, the mother of this brown and white dog was a bulldog. Her father was a beagle."

"Oh, she's very cute," Lou said. "Were these dogs rescued from somewhere?"

"Yes, they were. All of the dogs you see here used to live in very unsafe and unhealthy places. So we brought them out of those places so they could meet nice people and find safe homes."

This made Lou very sad. He really wanted to help one of these dogs. "It seems like a very hard life," he said to himself.

The woman pointed to a small brown dog curled up on a pillow in the corner of the tent. "That dog used to live with a pack of twenty-six wild dogs! She is very shy and quiet. She does not bark or jump or growl. She was probably one of the weakest dogs in the pack."

Lou walked over to the small brown dog and bent down to pet her. She let Lou pet her, but she was afraid. She had a very sweet face.

"What kind of dog is she?" Lou asked.

"She is a mix between a chocolate lab and a pit bull," the woman said.

This made Lou nervous. "I have heard that pit bulls are very mean," Lou said. He was afraid the dog would bite him.

"Many people think that pit bulls are mean," the woman said. "But they are only dangerous if their owners train them to be mean. As you can see, this dog is very gentle and kind."

At that moment, Lou decided he wanted to adopt the brown dog. He named her "Freedom" because she was now free from the hard and scary life she had as a member of the pack. She was free to be a happy and healthy dog. Lou loved Freedom right away.

Over the next four months, Lou and Freedom learned to live together. Lou thought Freedom was the sweetest dog he had ever known.

Lou saw that loud noises, new people, fast movements, and many other things scared Freedom. Lou helped Freedom understand that he was not going to hurt her. He talked quietly to her, petted her gently, and took her on walks every day. Slowly, Freedom learned to trust and love Lou.

One sunny afternoon, Lou hooked Freedom's leash to her collar and they walked outside to meet the mailman. When the mailman got closer, one of his packages fell on the sidewalk and made a very loud noise.

The loud noise scared Freedom. She jumped away from the box and the mailman. Before Lou could calm Freedom down, she ran into the street. Lou was still holding her leash. Then, very suddenly, a van drove down the street and hit Freedom.

The van stopped and the driver got out quickly. "I'm so sorry!" he said. "I did not see your dog coming!"

Freedom jumped up quickly, wriggled out of her collar, and began running. Lou called her name, but within one minute, Freedom was out of sight. Lou was very upset.

Lou thought it would be best for him to stay home in case Freedom decided to run back home. The man in the van wanted to help find Freedom, so he drove in the direction she had run, calling "Freedom!" out of his window.

There were many people walking and riding their bikes in Lou's neighborhood that afternoon. They could see that Lou was very upset, and he told them what happened. Quickly, the news spread all over the neighborhood. People that Lou knew and even people he did not know were looking for Freedom.

Lou decided he could not wait at home any longer. As he was unlocking his bike, another neighbor told Lou that he should call the dog warden. "The dog warden helps to protect and control all the dogs in town.

If anyone has found Freedom, they will probably call the dog warden first," she said.

"Great idea, thanks!" said Lou. He ran back inside and looked up the phone number for the dog warden and called. But he was too upset to explain the problem clearly.

The person on the phone said, "Calm down, sir. There is a report of a hurt dog in your neighborhood. The dog is actually at the emergency room at OSU Hospital."

Lou did not live far from OSU hospital. He hopped on his bike and rode there as fast as he could.

At the entrance of the emergency room, Lou propped his bike against the building. But a police officer stopped him.

"Sir, you can't leave you bike here," said the officer.

"I'm trying to get into the emergency room to see my dog! She was hit by a car, and she's in there. I don't have time to find a bike rack!" Lou said.

The police officer looked confused. He said, "Sir, this is a *people* hospital."

Lou told the officer that he knew this was a people hospital, but the dog warden told him that his dog was here. So the officer said Lou could leave his bike there until he checked on his dog.

Lou ran into the emergency room. "I'm here for my dog," he said to the first nurse he saw.

"Oh, yes, she's right over here," the nurse said kindly. He led Lou to the private room where they had taken Freedom.

Lou was shocked by what he saw when he walked into the room. Freedom was on a bed and she was shaking very badly. There were doctors and nurses standing around her. They were petting her and saying things to calm her down.

Lou noticed a lot of blood all over the room. He walked over to Freedom and saw that a piece of the van that hit her was stuck in her chest. This made Lou so upset that his stomach hurt.

"Sir, we are so sorry we could not do more to help your dog. We are not allowed to treat animals in this hospital. It is against the law. That is why we called the dog warden," said one doctor, who felt very sorry for Freedom and Lou.

Another doctor said, "It is amazing that she ran to the emergency room. She could have gone anywhere, but she ran here. You have a very special dog."

Lou thanked the nurses and doctors. When he picked up Freedom, her blood soaked into his clothes. But Lou didn't care. He just wanted to get his dog the help she needed.

As Lou was carrying Freedom out of the emergency room, the police officer who spoke with him earlier saw how badly Freedom was hurt. He felt very sorry for Lou and his dog.

"Excuse me, sir, where are you taking your dog?" the officer asked.

"To my vet in Clintonville," Lou said.

"You can't carry that dog on your bike!" the officer said. In all the confusion, Lou hadn't thought through how he was going to get Freedom to the vet.

"I can drive you to the OSU Veterinary Hospital. They treat hurt animals, and it is just down the road. You can put your bike in my trunk," said the officer.

"Thank you!" Lou said. He put Freedom in the back seat of the police car as gently as he could. There was blood all over. Then he threw his bike in the trunk. The police officer turned on his car lights and sirens.

When they got to the vet hospital, Lou thanked the officer for his help and carried Freedom inside.

The officer unloaded Lou's bike and leaned it against the building.

Everyone turned and looked at Lou and Freedom when they walked in. They were both covered in blood. Freedom was barely moving.

A man jumped across the counter and quickly, but gently, took Freedom out of Lou's arms. He took her back to a room where he could look at all the places on her body that were hurt.

After thirty minutes, the vet walked back into the waiting room.

"Your dog is going to live," said the vet. "She lost a lot of blood and she will need surgery. She also lost the pads on her front paws. But she will live."

"Okay, thank you," said Lou. He sat in the waiting room for a long while. He was feeling so many things. He felt very thankful that Freedom would live. He felt very sad because Freedom had been hurt so badly. He also felt very tired.

Then Lou remembered that he did not have his wallet with him. He would have to pay for Freedom's surgery, so he decided to ride home to get his wallet.

When he returned to the vet hospital later a woman looked at him and began crying. "I'm so sorry about your dog!" she said. Tears were coming down her cheeks.

"Thank you," Lou said. "I am hoping for the best. The vet said she needs surgery but she will live."

"Your dog is alive?" The woman looked confused. "I saw you leave the hospital. I thought you left because they could not save her. I thought your dog died," the woman said. She was wiping tears from her face.

"Oh, no," said Lou. "I had to go home to get my wallet. But I am thankful for your sympathy. Everyone has been so kind to me today. I am so grateful." Then Lou told the woman what happened that day.

As he told her the story, he remembered how many people had been kind to him.

He told her about the people in his neighborhood who looked for Freedom. He told her about the police officer, doctors, nurses, and vets who helped him.

So many people stopped what they were doing to help Lou and Freedom that day. That is why Lou calls this day "A Day of Kindness."

Today, Freedom is a healthy and happy dog. She loves to go for car rides and snuggle up with Lou. Lou likes to snuggle up with Freedom, too. Then he gives her kisses on the nose.

What Do You Think?

1. Freedom had a very hard life before she met Lou. How do you feel when you hear about an animal that is sick or hurt?

2. In the story, a lot of people helped Lou when Freedom ran away. Who are some of the people who helped Lou?

3. What does it mean to be kind?

4. When was someone kind to you? When were you kind to someone?

Tornado at Big Burger

Cast of Characters:

1. Brooke
2. Ben
3. Phil
4. Pam
5. Paul
6. Kyle
7. Sarah
8. Sam

There is also a Narrator. This person tells the readers what the characters are doing. The narrator reads all *italicized*, or *slanted*, words.

<u>Narrator</u>: *This is a play, which is a story that can be acted out on stage. This play happens in a restaurant called Big Burger.*

Inside Big Burger there are six people. Three are working behind the counter: Phil, Pam, and Paul. An older couple (Brooke and Ben) is looking at the menu. One man (Kyle) is sitting in the corner of the restaurant eating his food.

Outside Big Burger, two people (Sarah and Sam) have just parked their car and are walking into the restaurant. The weather outside is hot, humid, and windy. The sky is a strange yellow color.

<u>Brooke</u>: I don't know if I want a cheeseburger or a chicken sandwich.

<u>Ben</u>: Order the cheeseburger, Brooke. Every time you try something different, you always wish you had ordered the cheeseburger.

<u>Brooke</u>: Yes, you are right. But I think I will get a salad instead of fries.

<u>Ben</u>: Great, now you will eat half of my fries!

<u>Brooke</u>: Ha, ha.

<u>Narrator</u>: *Brooke and Ben step up to the register to place their orders. Just then, the front door of Big Burger opens with a "whoosh" sound. It is very windy outside.*

Two people (Sam and Sarah) walk inside. They are very windblown. Sarah smooths down her hair as she and Sam walk to the register and get in line behind Brooke and Ben.

<u>Phil</u>: Wow, it looks like the weather is getting pretty bad out there.

<u>Narrator</u>: *Brooke and Ben turn around and look out the windows. Tree branches are bending in the wind. Trash and leaves are swirling around. The sky and the clouds are turning dark.*

Brooke: It sure does. Maybe we should just go home, Ben.

Ben: No, we are already here. Let's just order and eat fast. [Ben looks at Phil.] Okay, we will have two cheeseburger meals, one with a side salad and root beer, and the other with fries and iced tea.

Brooke [elbowing Ben in the side]: Remember, no onions.

Ben: Oh, that's right, no onions on either burger, please.

Phil: Okay, your order is two cheeseburger meals, no onions on either burger. One meal has a salad and root beer and the other has fries and an iced tea. The total is $11.89.

Narrator: *Brooke pulls money out of her purse to pay for the food. In the back of the restaurant, Pam and Paul start making the cheeseburger meals. Sarah and Sam walk up to the register.*

Phil [looking at Sarah and Sam]: Hi, guys! Good to see you. I don't think I've seen you in Big Burger for a couple weeks.

Sarah: We were on vacation. We went to see the Grand Canyon!

Phil: Wow, I've never been there. I would love to see it.

Sam: It is amazing. It's so much bigger than you can even imagine. You should really try to get there. You would like it. Well, I'm starving! I think I will have the chicken finger meal with fries and lemonade.

Sarah: I'll have the usual, please. Plain hamburger and chocolate shake.

Phil: Okay, that will be $9.79.

Narrator: *Sam pays for their food. He and Sarah smile at Ben and Brooke, who are also waiting for their food. Phil walks to the kitchen to help Pam and Paul cook the food.*

Pam: We are almost finished with the first order. Can you make the chocolate shake, Phil?

Phil: Sure.

Narrator: *Paul walks from the kitchen to the register and looks outside. The wind is still blowing very hard and the sky is getting darker.*

Paul: Gosh, it sure is windy! I am surprised the wind did not blow your tiny car off the road on your way here!

Sarah and Sam [at the same time]: It almost did!

Narrator: *Kyle hears the people at the cash register talking about the wind. He gets up from his seat to check on his bicycle, which he rode to Big Burger. It is banging back and forth in the bike rack.*

Kyle [to Paul]: Would it be okay if I bring my bike inside while I finish my meal? I think the wind might blow it away!

Paul: Sure, go ahead.

<u>Narrator</u>: *Pam and Phil walk to the counter with Brooke and Ben's food.*

<u>Brooke</u> [to Ben]: You're right, I'm glad I got a cheeseburger.

<u>Narrator</u>: *Brooke and Ben walk to a table with their food. As they sit down, Kyle opens the door to bring his bike inside. When the door opens, everyone feels a big gust of wind. The napkins on Brooke and Ben's tray are blown to the floor.*

Kyle: It looks pretty bad out there, everyone. The sky is a weird yellow-purple color. And the clouds look dark and ugly.

Sam: I should go get my camera!

Sarah: No way. Let's just eat our food and get home.

Narrator: *Phil hands Sarah the tray with their food on it. Just then, everyone hears the tornado siren begin to wail. It sounds like a crying baby.*

Brooke [very scared]: Ben, I told you we should have gone home!

Ben: We live fifteen minutes away. We would still be in the car, and that is no place to be during a tornado.

Narrator: *Phil, Pam, and Paul walk out from behind the counter.*

Phil [speaking loudly to the five customers in the restaurant]: As you can hear, that is the tornado siren. You have two choices. You can join the Big Burger employees in the women's restroom—

that is our safe place during a tornado—or you must leave the restaurant.

<u>Sam</u>: Can we just eat really quickly and then leave?

<u>Sarah</u> [to Sam]: Seriously, I don't think I can eat in a public restroom!

<u>Pam</u>: Sorry, that is the rule. Paul and Phil and I have to go into the restroom during a tornado siren. Customers can choose to leave, or they can choose to go to the restroom with us.

There are too many glass windows in the dining area and it is not safe during bad weather. You can leave your food out here if you want to.

Narrator: *Right then, one of the large, plastic trash cans outside Big Burger falls over, hits the door, and starts rolling around in the parking lot.*

Ben: Whoa! Look at that! The sign for the office building across the street just blew over!

Narrator: *A large aluminum sign hits the ground with a loud clang. The wind blows it down the street. Its sharp corners look dangerous.*

Phil [looking worried]: Let's go, everyone.

Narrator: *The customers walk quickly into the women's restroom behind the Big Burger employees. Sam grabs his food and Sarah's food on the way.*

Narrator: *The restroom at Big Burger has brown tile floors and white tile walls. There are two stalls with toilets and one sink. It is very crowded with all the customers and employees trying to find room.*

<u>Brooke</u>: So, what now? Do we crouch down like we used to during tornado drills in school?

<u>Sarah</u>: There's no way I'm going to crouch down in a public restroom! I've already lost my appetite for this hamburger.

<u>Sam</u>: If you don't want it, I'll eat it.

<u>Narrator</u>: *Sarah hands Sam her burger. He takes a big bite and smiles at her.*

<u>Sarah</u>: I don't know how you can eat in a situation like this!

<u>Narrator</u>: *Sam shrugs his shoulders while he chews on Sarah's burger.*

<u>Paul</u>: Phil, do we have to crouch down? I don't remember what they said during the new employee training.

<u>Phil</u>: Hmmm, I don't think they told us what we were supposed to do once we were inside the restroom.

Besides, there is not much room in here. It would be tough for all of us to crouch down.

Pam: Okay, let's stand. Gosh, that siren is loud. It is making me nervous!

Kyle: Me too! I have always hated sirens. It means something bad is happening. When I was a kid I used to go hide under my parents' bed when I heard a siren.

Pam: I've always hated sirens, too. We need something to distract us.

Narrator: *There is a loud sound outside the restroom. It sounds like something very big hit one of the windows. Everyone in the restroom is scared by the noise.*

Ben: Man, I hope that wasn't one of our cars hitting the window!

Narrator: *Everyone laughs nervously, imagining a car hitting the window.*

Brooke: I know what we can do for distraction. My friend has a book that asks lots of questions like, "If you could go anywhere on vacation, where would you go?" Or, "If you could be a famous athlete, what sport would you play?"

Phil [looking at Brooke]: Great idea. How about you? If you could go anywhere on vacation, where would you go?

Brooke: That's easy. I have always wanted to go to Italy and see the Coliseum, where the people called gladiators used to fight lions. What about you?

Phil: I've never been to New York City. I think I'd like to go there.

Sam: Oh, New York City is wonderful, especially at Christmas time. Sarah and I love to travel. We do it as often as we can.

Sarah: That's right. Our next stop is Vermont to watch the changing leaves in the fall.

Paul: That sounds nice. I have never been outside this great state of Oklahoma.

Sam: What a bummer!

Paul: Oh, I don't mind. I like to be home. Besides, I tend to get sick in cars.

Kyle: Okay, I have a question for everyone. If you could be any animal, what kind would you be?

Ben [to Brooke]: Brooke, did we remember to shut the garage door?

Brooke: Yes, we did. [Brooke looks back to the group.] And if Ben could be any animal in the world, he would be a mule. He is as stubborn as a mule!

Narrator: *Everyone laughs at Brooke's joke.*

Pam: I would love to be a duck or some other kind of bird. I would love to fly!

Paul: Good answer, Pam. I think I would like to be a dog. Everyone loves dogs.

All they have to do is eat and lie around and let people pet them. What could be better?

Narrator: *The group hears a very loud crashing sound outside the restroom. The lights go out and it sounds like a roaring train is going by, but there are no train tracks near Big Burger.*

Phil [screaming]: Yikes! This is definitely a tornado!

Paul [screaming]: What?!

Narrator: *It is too loud to hear each other speak. Everyone gathers close together. Pam begins to cry. Sarah reaches out and squeezes Pam's hand. After thirty seconds, the noise stops.*

Ben: Is everyone okay?

Phil: I'm fine. Paul and Pam, are you okay?

Paul and Pam [quietly, at the same time]: Yes.

Narrator: *Sarah and Sam give each other a hug. Brooke places her hand on Kyle's shoulder.*

Brooke [to Kyle]: Are you okay?

Kyle: I think so. Thank you. I hope my bike is alright.

Brooke: Do you think we can leave the restroom now?

Sam: I think the storm has passed. Phil, are we allowed to leave the restroom?

Phil [thinking for a moment]: Let me open the door first and make sure it's okay.

Narrator: *Phil slowly opens the restroom door and sticks his head out. The sun is shining. He waves his hand to let everyone know they can follow him into the dining room.*

Narrator: *One of the large windows in the front of the restaurant is broken, and a large tree branch is sticking halfway through it. Kyle finds his bike, lying on its side. He picks it up. It is not damaged.*

Phil: Well, we have no electricity and a tree in the dining room. Not too bad! I expected it to be worse. [He looks relieved.]

<u>Brooke</u>: I should check on our car.

<u>Sam</u>: Good idea. Sarah, let's see if our little car is still out there.

<u>Narrator</u>: *Brooke, Sarah, and Sam walk over to a window to look at their cars. The parking lot is full of papers and cups and other trash. Many twigs and leaves are in the parking lot too. Some larger tree branches are broken and hanging down to the ground.*

Sarah: It is here, but one of the headlights is broken. [Sarah frowns at the broken headlight.] I wonder what did that.

Sam: Who knows? Maybe that shoe over there.

Narrator: *Everyone laughs as Sam points to a shoe in the parking lot.*

Paul: I'm just really happy that we are all okay and that no one got hurt!

Pam: Me too!

Narrator: *The Big Burger employees walk around to look at the napkins, ketchup packets, glasses and plates, and other small things that were blown all over the restaurant. They are careful to avoid the broken glass.*

Phil [talking to the customers]: Everyone, please be careful on your way home. Don't go near any power lines that might have been knocked down. We want to see you back at Big Burger as soon as we get the place cleaned up!

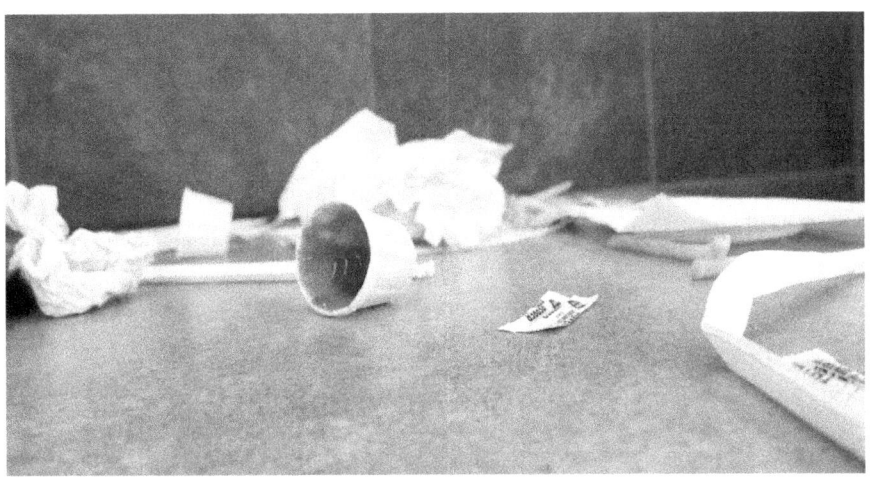

Narrator: *Everyone says thank you to Phil for giving them shelter from the tornado. They all promise to come back to Big Burger very soon.*

Ben [to Kyle]: Can we give you a ride home? We could put your bike in the back of our car.

Kyle: Yes, that would be great. Thank you!

Sam: Take care, everyone! [Sam looks as Sarah.] Sarah, do you have any of your chocolate shake left? I'm still hungry.

What Do You Think?

1. This story is a play. What is a play? Have you ever been to a play?

2. In the play, Sarah and Sam are "regulars" at Big Burger, which means they eat there a lot. Do you have a favorite place to eat? What do you like about it?

3. How would you feel if you were in a tornado like the people in Big Burger?

4. If you were at home and you heard a tornado siren, what would you do?

5. What kind of weather do you like?

Sneezes

Katie and Ed work together at a deli called Pastrami. Katie keeps things neat and clean and helps get the deli ready for business each day. Ed cuts and weighs all the meat and cheese and vegetables for the deli sandwiches.

"Ahh chooo!" Ed sneezed again.

"Bless you *again*," said Katie. "You keep sneezing. I hope I don't catch a cold from you!"

"Don't worry, I always cover my mouth with my sleeve when I sneeze. Besides, you wash your hands so much, you couldn't catch a cold if you tried," Ed replied. He stuck his tongue out at Katie.

Katie stuck her tongue out at Ed. She knew Ed was only joking around. They have become friends over the past few months. But when she first started working at the deli with Ed, it was a different story.

At first, Katie didn't think that Ed liked her because he called her "persnickety." Katie didn't know what this meant, so she talked with her job coach, Gus.

Gus thought that Ed was probably teasing Katie, because she *was* very thorough and focused on details. She spent a lot of time setting up the tables and chairs, filling the salt and pepper shakers, and neatly stacking the sandwich wrappers.

When Katie asked Ed why he called her persnickety, she realized that he was complimenting her on the tidiness of the deli's dining room. Ed said that he would stop calling her persnickety, but Katie decided that she liked this new word.

Ever since then, Katie and Ed have been friends. They pass the work hours before the deli opens by teasing each other…and working, of course!

"Well, I haven't missed a day of work since I started here eight months ago. You have missed five days of work. Washing my hands keeps me from getting sick. You should wash your hands more," said Katie.

"I wash my hands all the time, silly goose! Plus, I always wear gloves when I handle the meat and cheese," Ed said. "It's just allergies anyway. Every spring I sneeze and cough and feel stuffed up."

"So, can I stop saying 'bless you' when you sneeze? I have already said 'bless you' nine times this morning." Katie had been counting sneezes. She was very good at remembering numbers.

"Sure, but if you sneeze, I'm not going to say 'bless you' either." Ed was smiling as he turned to see Katie carefully filling the pepper shakers with pepper. "Have fun filling those pepper shakers," Ed laughed. He knew that pepper often makes people sneeze.

"That's just fine, I don't plan on sneezing. You're the one with...ah...ah...ah chooo...allergies. Oh great, now I just sneezed!"

Ed laughed.

A few days later, Ed was sneezing a little less. But now, he had a sore throat and a cough.

Katie noticed that Ed wasn't as happy or talkative as usual. She didn't like that. She thought Ed should go to the doctor. But when she told him so, he would say, "It's just allergies."

One morning, as Katie greeted Ed, she noticed that he looked very tired. "Are you okay?" she asked.

"I am. I'm just tired. I didn't get any sleep last night because I couldn't stop coughing. These allergies are getting old. And why is it so hot in here?" Ed asked.

"It's not hot, it's cold!" Katie said.

"Hmmm, whatever you say Persnickety Pattie," Ed said. But he decided to go check the thermostat to see how hot it was in the deli. Katie was right, it was cold. Why was he so hot? He wondered if he had a fever.

Then he wondered who would prepare the meat and cheese for the busy lunch rush if he went home. So he decided to stay and "tough it out," as his father would say.

An hour later, the deli was about to open. Ed had only cut half the meat and cheese he was supposed to. He was feeling very tired. He was thinking about how nice it would be to lie down on the bench by the front door and go to sleep.

Just then, Ed and Katie's manager, Sofia, walked into the deli. "Wow, Ed. You're running a bit behind this morning! Is everything okay?" Sofia asked.

"Yes, I'm fine. Sorry, I'm working more slowly than usual this morning," Ed said. He placed a large pile of provolone cheese in the deli case. "If you could hand me..." Ed began to say, but he started coughing and couldn't stop.

He knew how important it was not to cough next to any of the food. So he walked away from the deli counter and sat down at a table.

Katie looked up from the window she was cleaning. This cough sounded painful. In fact, Ed looked like he was in pain. "Ed, you are sick," she said.

Sofia walked over to Ed and placed her hand on his forehead. "Holy cow! You're burning up! You need to leave. I'd head straight to the doctor if I were you!" Sofia said.

"I can't leave. What about the rest of the turkey and Swiss cheese?" Ed asked.

"Let me worry about the turkey and cheese. You're too sick to be at work!" Sofia wanted the deli to be ready for the lunch rush. But she knew it was more important for Ed to get better.

"Okay, okay, I'll go. But don't forget we need extra...ah choo! Swiss cheese for today's sandwich special," Ed said as Sofia was pushing him out the door.

"Katie and I have it covered. Now go!" Sofia shut the door behind Ed and turned to look at Katie. "You seem to have things finished out here in the dining room. Can you help me load the deli case?"

"I haven't done that before, but I think I can," Katie replied. Katie got nervous. She thought about calling her job coach, Gus, but there wasn't enough time. She would have to start a new task without Gus's help.

Sofia began cutting the rest of the turkey. She asked Katie to go to the refrigerator to get the big block of Swiss cheese on the second shelf.

Katie walked down the hallway to the refrigerator. She opened the big, heavy door. The refrigerator was big enough for two people to fit inside! There was a lot of food in there.

Katie looked around and saw ham, roast beef, salami, tomatoes, onions, pickles, cheddar cheese, provolone cheese…by now Katie had forgotten what Sofia asked her to get! Was it provolone cheese? Or was it mozzarella cheese?

Katie got nervous again. She didn't want to bring Sofia the wrong cheese. Should she take a guess? Then she had an idea.

Katie remembered that the cheese was for today's special sandwich. All she had to do was go to the dining room and look at the whiteboard that said "Today's Special." Everything on the sandwich would be listed there.

Katie walked into the dining room, past the kitchen where Sofia was cutting turkey. Sofia spotted Katie and asked, "Hey Katie! Did you bring the cheese with you?"

Katie stopped and said, "Um, not yet. I'm sorry, I forgot what kind of cheese you wanted. I was going to look at the whiteboard because it is the cheese on today's special sandwich."

Sofia said, "Great idea. While you are looking, can you tell me what kind of bread we need for the sandwich? I forget!"

Katie smiled. She felt relieved. She had been afraid that Sofia would be upset with her, but instead, Katie was now able to help Sofia with something she forgot. Katie decided to read all the sandwich ingredients out loud, in case they forgot anything else.

"'Ed's Onion Delight: Enjoy fresh-sliced turkey piled high on an onion bagel with Swiss cheese, bacon, tomato, lettuce, and onions. Ed suggests our sour cream and onion chips on the side.' Gosh, Ed must like onions a lot!" Katie said to Sofia.

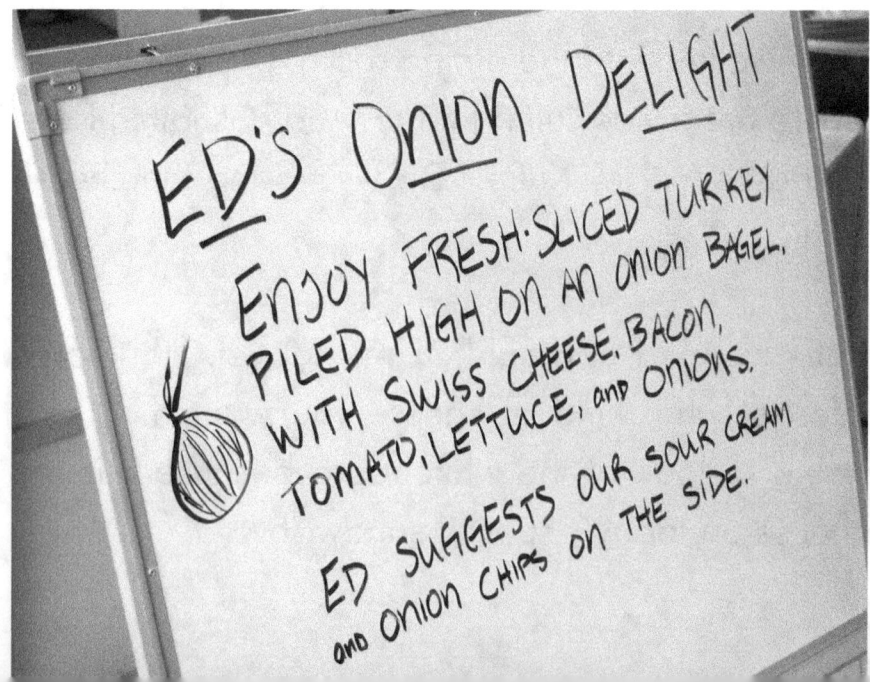

"I think you're right! I'm not a fan of onions. What about you, Katie?" Sofia asked.

"No, I don't like them. They make my breath smell bad," Katie answered.

"Yes, they can do that. Maybe we'll give one of those red and white peppermints to anyone who orders the special today," Sofia said. She smiled at Katie, who was on her way back to the refrigerator to get the Swiss cheese.

Katie smiled back and said, "Great idea! I'll bring a bag of mints from the storage closet after I get the Swiss cheese."

"Thank you, Katie," Sofia said. Katie walked happily down the hallway to the refrigerator.

Ed called later and said that he would need the next three days off work. The doctor told him he had an infection in his lungs. He would need to take medicine to get better. Katie and Sofia were glad they made Ed go to the doctor.

"I will come in early the next few days to fill in for Ed," Sofia told Katie. "Maybe you can help me a little? I'm not as fast as Ed."

Katie smiled and said, "I would be happy to help." Katie looked forward to learning new things at work. She decided that Pastrami was the best place in the world to work.

What Do You Think?

1. What does it feel like just before you sneeze? What does it feel like after you sneeze?

2. In the story, Ed resists going to the doctor. Have you ever done this? Why?

3. In the story, Katie has a job coach to help her learn her job at the deli. Have you ever had someone like a job coach help you learn a new job?

4. Katie was nervous to help Sofia with Ed's job. Do you ever feel nervous when someone asks you to try something you've never done before? Why?

5. If you could work anywhere, where would you work?

About the Authors:

Dr. Tom Fish is Director of Social Work at the Ohio State University Nisonger Center on Disabilities where he directs programs focused on community inclusion, adult literacy, autism, and sibling support. A Fellow of the American Association on Intellectual and Developmental Disabilities, Dr. Fish is also a founding member of the National Sibling Leadership Network, and a board member of the Down Syndrome Association of Central Ohio. He has three great adult children.

Jillian Ober has worked at The Ohio State University Nisonger Center on Excellence in Developmental Disabilities since 2004. At Nisonger Center, Jillian manages and disseminates programs that emphasize community inclusion and lifelong learning for people with intellectual and developmental disabilities. One such program is the Next Chapter Book Club, which offers weekly opportunities for people with a wide range of abilities to read, learn, and socialize in community settings. Jillian received both her undergraduate and graduate degrees (Psychology, Rehabilitation Counseling) from The Ohio State University.